For CANDY STRIPERS—Everywhere!

With a special thank you to my own be-starred daughter, Jane, Volunteer at the Morristown Memorial Hospital; and to Judy and Sue Avery, who really started it all; and to these New Jersey directors of volunteers: Mrs. Mary Brady, All Souls' Hospital, Morristown; Miss Elizabeth Brinley, Morristown Memorial; Mrs. Dorothy Mosher, Overlook Hospital, Summit; Miss Edith W. Johnson, Mountainside Hospital, Montclair. Also, to Mrs. Olive Dutton, R.N., charged with in-service training at Memorial Hospital, for checking technical points; Sister Mary Eleanor, R.N., administrator of All Souls' Hospital; to Miss Elin Nelson, in charge of the Clinic at Memorial, and the countless girls, "Pink Ladies," nurses, doctors and interns who not only answered my questions, but allowed me to work beside them and in their areas, at first as an interested observer and then as a confirmed Volunteer, having discovered how necessary such service is in the hospital family.

And last, but not least, to Miss "Denny," of the Morristown Library, tireless researcher, always ready to track down the smallest elusive fact in the library archives.

Gratefully,
Lee Wyndham

The Fold
Morristown, New Jersey

Author's Note

CANDY STRIPERS is a romance woven around the fascinating hospital field open to teen-age girls. It is in no way intended to portray real persons, or the exact workings of any hospital, but is a composite of information gathered and observed and turned to the fictional uses best suited to the ramifications of my plot.

"In no other act does man approach so near the gods as when he is restoring the sick to the blessings of health."

—CICERO.

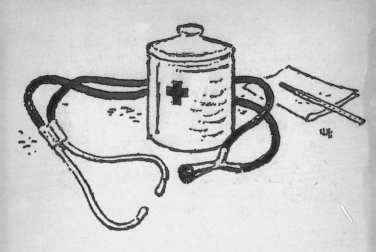

one

BONNIE SCHUYLER, BLONDE HAIR CAUGHT UP IN
a high pony tail, stomped out of the house and
glared at her mother's May garden without
seeing a single spring blossom. Hands behind
her back, she gripped her Latin II text as if she
intended to choke it instead of study for Monday's exam. Her eyes swept over the lawn, past
the badminton court freshly lined with marble
dust by her younger sister, Laura, and settled
on the hammock.

Her face softened. Muffin, the family's half-
Persian amber cat, was curled up in a sunlit
ball in the exact center of the hammock. She

1

moved toward him, and as he opened one golden brown eye, she scooped him up, turned, and still holding him, dropped into the hammock. Muffin yawned, settled himself more comfortably on his stomach and went back to sleep. Bonnie stroked his soft fur absently. Muffin's life, at any rate, was perfect, unlike her own.

First, her best friend, Anne Moore, who had lived next door, moved to Oregon. Bonnie still missed Anne dreadfully. The two girls had done everything together. They had joined the same clubs, gone to the same dancing school. When they had started going out with boys, more often than not it was on double dates. With Anne gone Bonnie felt as if she had been cut adrift. There was no one in Hamilton High who would make such a wonderful intimate friend as Anne had been. And they had made gorgeous plans for this summer at the shore, too, before the business of Anne's moving to Oregon had come up.

Late afternoon sun slanted under the tall ash trees into the hammock and Bonnie stretched her long slim legs in the warm rays. Looking over the amber-colored cat, she surveyed with disfavor the winter whiteness of her skin, visible below her shorts. Her legs wouldn't get much darker with the grim summer that lay ahead, she reflected, and sighed lugubriously.

Muffin stirred and made a soft, *"Murrow!"* of protest.

"Oh, hush," Bonnie said. "You have nothing to complain about. You don't realize that on top of everything else our beach house at the shore is going to be rented to strangers this summer! We've been going there every season for as long as I can remember, but this year we'll be staying right here, in Hamilton, New Jersey." She thrust out her lower lip in a pout.

It was all because of Father's old budget, Bonnie thought resentfully, and was instantly ashamed. "The Budget" was, after all, designed to protect the family, and her father imposed strict rules about it. This year a new car had become a must, and since funds he had been setting aside regularly for her future college education and Laura's had not been available, the beach house rental was the answer.

"That eight hundred dollars the New York people are willing to pay for the season will help a lot," Mr. Schuyler had informed his family. "You know, college for each of you girls will cost two thousand a year and then some. Multiplied by four years apiece that's a pretty staggering amount. But that money is going to be in the bank and on tap when you girls need it. I know all of you are disappointed about missing our usual summer at the shore, but it's not as though we lived in the city—and you know how important maintaining that fund is to me."

Yes, they knew, Bonnie thought, stroking Muffin's velvety ears. The fund had run short for her Dad years ago, and when a family emergency arose, he had to drop out of the university and change his career dreams entirely.

The thing with her, however, was that she had no special career dreams to cherish as yet. There were so many fields to choose from—and how was one to know, at fifteen, in what special direction her own, so far invisible talents lay? Mother thought she should consider teaching or library work. It was "safe," she said. Mother was forever trying to safeguard her daughters. People would always need teachers, and librarians were scarce. But Bonnie did not feel that she had any aptitude for either of these professions.

She rather envied the sure-footed young people who knew exactly where they were going; boys like Cliff Coburn, their new neighbor on the right, who had moved into Anne's house. Cliff lapped up math and science in preparation for engineering. Even her own sister, twelve-year-old Laura, she thought with wry amusement, seemed to be preparing to become a walking encyclopedia. Laura memorized and collected mountains of unassorted facts in a pack-rat nest of notebooks, folders and pamphlets that crowded her bookshelf allotment in their room and spilled over into Bonnie's neatly stacked, carefully chosen list of favorites.

The May sun was warm on her legs and it made her think of the coming summer again. "It might not be so gruesome if I could get a store job," she told the indifferent Muffin. She liked people, liked the sight of fresh new merchandise. Maybe she would be a buyer someday. It would be an exciting, glamorous career. But now, because of some silly regulations about insurance or something, no store in Hamilton would hire a person until she was at least sixteen. Bonnie would not be sixteen for almost a year. A year to wait. Forever!

This summer there would be no sailing and no swimming with the shore crowd. Bonnie thought longingly of the boys and girls she had come to know so well—of the clubhouse, where they held dances, and of the beach picnics. There would be no gorgeous suntan for her, either, the kind one acquired from hours and hours on the sand. Just baby-sitting—maybe. Again Bonnie sighed.

One nice family had wanted to take her with them to Cape Cod for a month, after they'd heard she would not be going away, but Mother would not hear of it. Bonnie was being treated like a child. An absolute *child!* At fifteen!

And to add injury to the insult, there would be no one at home this summer to have fun with. No boys. Rock Caldwell, Hamilton High's star athlete, who'd be her steady now if Mother and Daddy had not put up such a fuss, was going to be away all summer as counselor in a boys' camp. Even though they were not steadies, they went around a lot together, and the other fellows considered her Rock's girl. No one would date her. It would be a shoreless, dateless, horrid, dull, boring summer.

Bonnie shifted in the hammock and Muffin woke up and stared at her full of reproach. He switched his fluffy tail, leaped down to the ground and stalked away with a great show of dignity.

"All right. Leave me," Bonnie grumbled.

A rhythmic drumbeat made her turn her head to the right. Cliff Coburn was getting in a few licks before rushing off to one of his afternoon jobs, she supposed. She recalled how excited she had been when the tall, dark-haired boy moved in next door last winter. But the excitement had been wasted. Cliff had at once become involved in all sorts of school affairs, topmost among which was the swing band. He played a marvelous drum at the dances, besides helping to decorate the gym by stringing wires and inventing clever lighting effects. Cliff was going to be an electrical engineer. His sights were set for MIT, and although he was sure to get a scholarship with his grades, he had also taken on a variety of part-time jobs to help save up money for the additional expenses of his schooling. Every moment of his life was occupied—and girls had no place in his scheme of things. No girl had been able to make the slightest impression on him and Cliff steamed through the school halls with his eyes fixed always a few inches above all the other heads, his thoughts elsewhere.

Cliff was going to be around all summer—Laura had found that out. Laura, who was as friendly as a puppy and never took rebuffs seriously, had managed to get their neighbor to change her bike tire the other day and came back with a complete report on her "interview" with him. "I just asked him and he told me," she informed her appalled sister as she recounted Cliff's answers to her prying questions about himself, his past and his future, all of which seemed to involve a fantastic amount of work.

"I was *not* prying!" Laura denied hotly when Bonnie remonstrated with her. "I was interested. And anyway, it's very important to know how to interview people. I might decide to be a reporter. I asked Cliff didn't he like girls, because he never seemed to go out with any. That's what you said, wasn't it?"

"You didn't say *that!*" Bonnie shrieked.

"No, 'course not. Anyway, he said he didn't like girls if they were over twelve. They were too much trouble and wanted too much attention from a fellow. But I still had a year to go, providing my bike didn't need too much fixing." She laughed, as if this were the most humorous and witty thing she'd ever heard. "Cliff's not really good looking, but I think he's cute, and I love his crewcut," she added. "It's like a black brush on top of his head," and with this she flounced away.

In all the months Cliff had lived next door on Longview Avenue, Bonnie had never succeeded in getting more than an absent-minded "hello" from him. But then, *she* was over twelve!

Upstairs, at the Coburns', the drumbeats ceased. Bonnie dragged one foot listlessly as she swung in the hammock and scowled at the Mayblue sky.

"Whom are you trying to scare up there?" a laughing, feminine voice demanded, and Bonnie sat up with a jerk, her forgotten Latin book flying out of her lap.

Nancy Wheeler picked it up, and still laughing, restored it to Bonnie. She was a big, comfortable girl, and as usual, seemed to be bursting with health and good humor. Her brown hair was combed into a smooth pageboy, and her general air of wholesomeness was accentuated by the crisp white blouse and pink-striped uniform she wore.

The Wheelers were the Schuylers' neighbors on the left, but Bonnie had never been close friends with Nancy. For one thing, there was a two-year age difference between the girls, and for another, Nancy's interests were not the same as hers—and of course, there had been Anne. The Wheeler clan, all eight of them, lived in a huge old frame house which was always packed not only with the Wheelers, but with scores of their friends in assorted ages. The happy bedlam never failed to amaze Bonnie, but it did not seem to faze any of the Wheelers—Nancy and her mother least of all. They were always serene and bright-eyed and busy.

Nancy was a junior in Hamilton High and worked at the hospital after school, but what she did at the big new Medical Center was a mystery to Bonnie.

"Sorry I startled you," Nancy apologized. "I came out to cut a bouquet from Mother's iris border and saw you in the hammock. Are you mad at the world?"

Looking up at pink-cheeked, perfectly adjusted Nancy, it was impossible to stay "mad at the world," and Bonnie suddenly felt silly. Lying in a hammock and grousing was such an unconstructive way to face life—and more specifically, the coming summer.

Bonnie moved over and patted the place beside her. "Sit down, Nancy, and I'll tell you all about it," she said, and then, changing her mind, asked. "What are you going to do with yourself this summer?"

Nancy looked surprised. "Why, I'm going to work at the hospital as usual."

"You are?" Bonnie could not conceal her amazement. "You know, I've often wondered what on earth you do there."

"I'm a junior volunteer. A Candy Striper." Nancy smoothed her starched pinafore. "This is my uniform. As a matter of fact, I'm on my way for my Friday evening duty at the Clinic, as soon as the bus comes by," she glanced at her wrist watch, "in fifteen minutes. There are always a lot of emergencies on Fridays, and the hospital is shorthanded, especially on weekends."

"Emergencies!" Bonnie shuddered, picturing

gory accident victims. "How can you stand it? I mean—it must be awful sometimes."

"It is—sometimes," Nancy agreed gravely. "But knowing that you are helping people in trouble makes it easier to stand a lot of things. I make myself generally useful, helping nurses and doctors. I'm going to be a nurse, you know." Nancy's face glowed with quiet content.

"Yes, of course. You belong to the Future Nurses Club in school," Bonnie recalled, "and you've been a Candy Striper for a long time. At least I think I've seen you in this uniform for years."

"Two years, almost," Nancy said. She looked positively dedicated.

"I wish I knew what I'll be. It's so hard to decide. There are zillions of things. But my immediate problem is this summer. We're not going to the shore, and there's nothing—just nothing to do!"

Nancy studied her thoughtfully. "Why not become a Candy Striper?"

"But I don't know anything about taking care of sick people," Bonnie said.

Nancy smiled. "We think of them as people getting well. Besides, to quote our handbook, 'The duties of the Candy Stripers include only nonpersonal care.' We don't do anything *to* the patients, only *for* them. I mean, we don't give them baths or bedpans, or take temperatures. We're like junior nurse's aides. We do things that require no technical skill or special training, but help to make patients more comfortable and happy and save the nurses' time for the really important tasks. There's a new class being formed soon. Why don't you come in and see what it's all about?"

Bonnie pondered the suggestion. If she became a Candy Striper she would work at the hospital as a volunteer, without pay. But on the other hand, there seemed no likelihood of her getting any well-paying job anyway. At least this would give her something to *do*. She eyed Nancy's crisp uniform. It was cute. Bonnie imagined herself in it. With her small waist the full skirt would be very attractive.

"I'll do it," she announced impulsively. "Do I sign up or what?"

"You sign up. I'll make an appointment for your interview with Mrs. Brent—she's the Director of Volunteers. You'll have to get your parents' consent, of course, but that will be all right, won't it?"

The question dashed a wave of doubt over Bonnie. Her parents were so fussy about what she did, especially Mother. But this was, well, WORTHWHILE. She said the word to herself in capitals. Besides, Nancy was a Candy Striper,

and wasn't Mrs. Wheeler an adult Volunteer?
Bonnie began to marshal her points of argument. Perhaps she would have more facts to
present if she saw Mrs. Brent first. There
might be a brochure of some kind that she
could bone up on. She smiled, recalling how her
young sister backed her own arguments with
collected facts. She would borrow a leaf from
Laura's method.

"Of course!" she now said confidently.

Nancy glanced at her wrist watch and stood
up. Her bus was due.

"You make that appointment for me," Bonnie
said.

"All right. Will do." Nancy waggled her fingers and hurried away, her pink-striped pinafore rustling.

Bonnie settled back into the hammock for
some constructive thinking this time. Persuading her family, especially Mother, would take
some doing. One of Mother's major worries
was *germs*. She was so afraid of germs attack-
ing her children. And a hospital full of sick people! How would she react to that?

two

NANCY SET UP AN INTERVIEW FOR BONNIE
with the director of Volunteers for the very
next day—Saturday.

"Come over to the Medical Center at eleven," Nancy said, "and have me paged from the
Information Desk. I'll take you in and introduce you to Mrs. Brent."

Instead of spending the morning at the Record Shop with the high-school crowd, Bonnie
boarded the Longview Avenue bus and got off
in front of the new five-story Hamilton Medical Center. It was an imposing modern edifice of
brick and wide expanses of glass, facing a cir-

cular, tree-shaded drive and parking areas. Shaped like a huge, wide-open block letter Y, its wings reached out deep into the lawns on either side, and its long stem went back into the rear of the property. A nurses' residence was on the right, and behind it were utility buildings of some sort.

It was all very handsome and spic and span, and as Bonnie walked toward the main entrance, the steps flanked by wheel-chair ramps, she recalled some of the newspaper publicity which attended the opening of Hamilton's new community hospital. It was reported to have the newest in construction and design, the most up-to-date equipment. But, actually, Bonnie had no idea what a hospital was like inside, except for what she had seen in movies and on TV, and of course she'd read they always smelled of antiseptics. She pushed through the revolving door nervously. The muted coral and greens and the modern furniture of the lobby made her think of a hotel; and it did not smell. It was spacious and comfortable, and softly lit. There were landscape paintings on the walls. The floor tiles gleamed with polish. A number of people were sitting on leather-covered chairs and couches, reading newspapers or magazines, or talking quietly. They were obviously visitors.

Bonnie spotted a switchboard behind a glass

partition and the Information Desk next to it.
She gave her name to the pleasant woman in
the pink smock and asked for Nancy Wheeler.
A moment later she heard a soft voice broad-
casting the call for her friend. A telephone
rang and Bonnie was informed that Nancy
would be there directly. Soon she was standing
before her. How smoothly everything func-
tioned!

"You're right on time," Nancy said approvingly. "Mrs. Brent's office is this way."

Except for the occasional nurse in uniform,
this might be any business establishment, Bonnie thought as she accompanied Nancy down a
corridor, past offices and desks with busy secre-
taries tapping away at typewriters.

Mrs. Brent's office was not large, but it was
comfortably furnished with modern pieces and
lined with cabinets. One section of wall had a
fiber bulletin board on which hung an array of
round tags. On top of a low cabinet were two
thick record books, one labeled, "Volunteers,"
the other, "Candy Stripers."

An attractive, vital woman with thick wavy
brown hair drawn off the face into a high bun
looked up from a pile of papers and smiled
warmly as the girls approached her desk.

"Mrs. Brent," Nancy said, "this is Bonnie
Schuyler, my next-door neighbor."

Bonnie found herself being surveyed by a
pair of lively blue eyes which, for all their
friendliness, seemed not to miss a single detail
about her. She was suddenly glad that she had
not worn her customary Saturday Bermudas
and bulky socks, but instead had selected a neat
tailored cotton dress, topped by a spotless
white sweater.

The Director of Volunteers reached out and
took Bonnie's hand in a firm clasp. "How do you
do, Bonnie. I understand you'd like to be a volunteer. Sit down and tell me about yourself."
She waved toward a chair and glanced at
Nancy. "You may go back to the Clinic. I'm
sure they need you."

Nancy nodded, smiled reassuringly at Bonnie
and disappeared.

"She is one of our very best and most dependable volunteers," Mrs. Brent remarked.
"A wonderful girl. Now, Bonnie, what year are
you in school? And how old are you?" She asked
a number of general questions, jotting down
Bonnie's answers on a card, and then chatted
with her for five minutes more, taking stock of
the new applicant. "We're having an unprece-
dented response to our call for summer volunteers." She then said, "I'm afraid we won't be
able to use all the girls, especially those whose
applications come in late. Here is a blank for

you to fill out. This must be signed by your parent or guardian. And this is a booklet of rules, regulations, and duties of Candy Stripers. You'll want to study it before you fill out preference for work areas and consider the time you'll have to give to the Center. Mail this back to me." Mrs. Brent seemed to be smiling dismissal without committing herself in any way.

Bonnie took the application blank and brochure, said good-by and left, feeling rather shaken. All the preliminaries made this seem like such serious business, more serious than anything she had ever been engaged in before. She had not taken up Nancy's suggestion about becoming a Candy Striper in quite that sober a mood, but now she realized that this was indeed a grown-up world she would become involved in; and for just a moment she wondered if she really wanted to be accepted.

But on her way out of the hospital she saw several pert Candy Stripers flitting in and out of the elevators and walking through the corridors, swiftly and surely. They had an air of belonging to the Center, of having purpose and direction, and all at once Bonnie wanted purpose and direction, too, instead of the rudderless summer she might otherwise have.

What sort of an impression had she made on Mrs. Brent? Had the Director of Volunteers

considered her a sensible, responsible person?
Dependable? Like Nancy? Well, of course,
everyone couldn't be as devoted as Nancy. . . .

Bonnie saw the bus approaching and raced
to the stop. Finding a seat in the rear she began
to look over the papers Mrs. Brent had given
her. Here was the "Parental Permission" slip.

I hereby give permission for my daughter

_____

Date of birth_____

to become a member of the Junior Aides.
I understand that the work to be done at the
Hamilton Medical Center will include only
nonpersonal duties such as: delivering mail,
doing errands to the laboratory, X-ray De-
partment, or Central Supply; also arrang-
ing flowers, stacking linen, serving nourish-
ment trays, etc.; as well as doing specific
pieces of work designated by the floor super-
visor.

I understand that my daughter will be
working as a Volunteer at the hospital.

_____Parent
_____Address
_____Telephone

Well, that didn't seem too complicated or dangerous. There was nothing here to upset her mother.

The Manual for Junior Aides detailed the work more fully. There was a great deal to do, and many departments in which a Candy Striper could be useful, from the business office to floor duty, and even in the clinic, where experienced girls were used. Bonnie studied the booklet with mounting interest.

Unlike most girls, she had never played nurse, nor had she steeped herself in the adventures of *Sue Barton* or the other fictional nurses, but now she found herself feeling "nursish." She had to smile at that. Hospitals, after all, were "contagious." She'd been exposed to the atmosphere of the Center so briefly, and already she had caught the urge to become a part of its orderly routine.

Now to tackle Mother and Dad! Oops, she had almost gone beyond her bus stop. She scrambled to her feet and hurried to the exit.

Lunch was already on the table and the family were about to sit down when Bonnie burst into the house.

"Wash your hands, dear," Mother said, "and come right in."

Bonnie left her application and manual on the hall table near the telephone and ducked into the kitchen. The soap guaranteed to kill twenty-seven germs was lying in the soap dish as usual. She let it do its work and then joined the family.

The sun, streaming in through the dining-room windows, made a shining helmet of her mother's ash blonde hair. She was pleasantly rounded and pretty, and very much concerned with the welfare of her family. Dad was tall and rather distinguished looking, with an air of calm reasonableness about him. Just what Mother needed on occasion, Bonnie thought as she slid into place. Her sister Laura, short, curly-haired, and still plagued by "baby fat," was already diving into her food, dimples playing in her cheeks as she ate—much too fast. Laura was always in a hurry to get somewhere.

Mother had prepared a nourishing, attractive lunch, but Bonnie was not hungry. She longed to plunge right in and tell them all about becoming a Candy Striper, but she knew the announcement might create tension and that would spoil lunch and put one mark against the project at the very start. She would have to wait until the meal was over.

The telephone bell jingled and Laura leaped up, nearly upsetting her chair. "That's for me! Dodie Wheeler is supposed to call me about playing tennis this afternoon."

Mother frowned. "Laura, you know I don't like telephone calls at mealtimes."

"Sorry, Mom. I forgot!" Laura's dimples flashed. She sounded chastened, but Bonnie knew her sister was unscathed by mild reprimands.

Laura returned looking puzzled. "Hey, what's this?" She was holding Bonnie's application and reading from the Manual: " 'Report to Head Nurse immediately. Ask for your assignment at the nursing desk . . . learn the routine expected of you and . . .' *Candy Striper's Manual!* Bonnie, is this yours?" she shrieked. "Are you going to be a Candy Striper? Why didn't you tell me?"

Bonnie could have cheerfully throttled her sister. "Because you didn't give me the chance!" The words came through gritted teeth. "Give me that!" She snatched the booklet and papers.

"Bonnie!" Mother was shocked. "Such manners. Perhaps you had better explain what this is all about."

Father set down his fork, wiped his lips with his napkin.

Bonnie swallowed painfully. This was not the way she had planned it. Laura looked contrite, realizing that she had let some secret cat out of the bag.

"I—I want to serve as a Candy Striper at the

Medical Center," Bonnie faltered, her cheeks flushed. "Be a junior volunteer aide."

"Good heavens!" Mother sounded as if Bonnie had announced she was planning to go over Niagara Falls in a paper bag. "Work in a hospital? Among all those sick people! The *germs!* Bonnie, wherever did you get such an idea?"

"Well, from Nancy to begin with. She's been a Candy Striper for almost two years—and no germs seem to have gotten to her!"

"I should say not!" Laura chimed in helpfully. "Nancy's strong as a horse."

"Precisely," Mother said. "Bonnie isn't."

Her elder daughter groaned. Ever since she'd had a touch of anemia, back in seventh grade, Mother fancied her to be delicate. "Oh, Mother!" she wailed. "Dad, for goodness sakes, tell Mother I'm not wasting away."

"Of course you're not." Father reached out and patted her hand soothingly. "Suppose we all listen to what you have to say about this—quietly." He really looked interested, Bonnie thought.

"I don't know too much about the work, yet," she said, taking heart. "But Nancy certainly enjoys it, and lots of other girls in school do it. I never thought about it until yesterday, when Nancy and I had a talk. Since I can't get a real job this summer, and since we are not going to the shore, I thought I might as well do something useful. It will be good experience."

"But suppose you catch something?"

"Oh, Mother, nurses don't go around catching things all the time. They always look so scrubbed and healthy—and I won't have nearly their contact with patients." Father was studying her thoughtfully, and she suddenly remembered a fact she'd overlooked. Dad had once wanted to be a doctor! That was the dream he'd had to give up.

He came to her rescue now. "Take it easy, Fran," he said to his wife. "Many hospitals use volunteers these days. They could not operate efficiently without them, and I'm sure the volunteers at Hamilton are protected. I know the Center has a Contagion Wing—Hartwell Pavilion—where people with communicable diseases are kept. I'm sure the volunteers do not go into that area."

"We could ask Nancy about it," Laura suggested

Her mother looked as if she thought that Nancy had done enough harm already. "Nancy *wants* to be a nurse," she said.

"And I don't know what I want to be," Bonnie replied, "except a Candy Striper this summer. I went to see Mrs. Brent, the Director of Volunteers, about it this morning, and she said they were getting more applicants than they will be able to use. Girls who apply late will be turned down, and I got the impression their standards are high. I'm not even sure I'll be able to get in."

This put another light on the subject and Bonnie saw her mother bridle at the suggestion that Mrs. Brent might not find *her* daughter suitable! Darling Mother was so transparent. Bonnie had to smile. Inspired, she said, "Mom, Mrs. Wheeler is a Volunteer. She certainly wouldn't have her daughter at the Center if there were anything wrong with it. Why don't you talk to Mrs. Wheeler? Please?" After all, Mom wasn't being obstinate. Her perpetual worries did stem from love for her children.

"An excellent suggestion," Mr. Schuyler agreed. "You do that, Fran. Right after lunch," he added, in case she thought next week might do, "while I get after the dandelions on the lawn."

"All right—but—"

"No buts," her husband said. "Didn't I see apple pie in the kitchen? A la mode, I hope?"

She was diverted, and lunch proceeded.

"I'll—" Laura began recklessly and then amended, *"we'll* wash the dishes, Mom. You go on over and see Mrs. Wheeler."

Twenty minutes dragged by.

"Oh, sugar," Laura said, putting the last dish away. "I have to go. Dodie's waiting for me."

Giving Bonnie a sympathetic hug, she disappeared, tennis racket in hand. Bonnie took up a post near a window where she could watch for her mother's return. In the middle of the lawn Muffin sat washing himself calmly, as if nothing crucial were being decided.

At last her mother emerged from the Wheeler house, and Dad at once stopped his attack on the dandelions and followed her back into the house.

Mother seemed slightly dazed. "That Pat Wheeler," she said, "is so full of enthusiasms, she overwhelms me. Goodness knows how she finds time for everything she does—with that brood of hers, and that enormous house."

"But what about the Volunteers?" Bonnie prompted.

"I'm coming to that. This Volunteer business is one of Pat's pet projects and she can't say enough for it. The grownups, by the way, are called Pink Ladies, because they wear pink smocks. To hear Pat talk, you'd think the Hamilton Memorial would close its doors without the Candy Stripers and the Pink Ladies."

"Then you'll let me join, if they'll have me?" Bonnie cried.

Her mother looked troubled. "I suppose so, but I hope you won't decide to become a nurse. It's such hard work, and——"

"Oh, *Mother!*" Bonnie threw her arms around her. "I just want to be a Candy Striper —this summer! I don't want to be a nurse." She whirled about, hugged her father, and then, picking up her application and the manual, raced toward the stairs.

"You know what Pat told me?" she heard her mother say to her father. "That when she became a Volunteer, she took out insurance against the years when her children would be grown up and gone and she would have nothing to do! Children set up such a racket for eighteen or twenty years, she said, and then they leave, and the silence is almost more than one can bear!"

Mother sounded so distressed that Bonnie stopped and turned. Father had his arms around her. "You're such a mother hen," he said. "You must realize your chicks have to go out and scratch on their own. It's a law of nature."

Bonnie took the stairs, two at a time, the application blank crackling in her hand.

three

A LETTER WAS TUCKED UNDER BONNIE'S DESK
reminder clip when she returned home from
school on Wednesday.

Dear Bonnie:

    *You have been accepted for probation as a
Candy Striper at the Hamilton Medical Center.*

    *A new training class begins at 10 A.M. on
Saturday, May 8th, in the Meeting Room on
the Fifth Floor.*

*You are most cordially welcomed, for we
need you in our hospital family.*
                              Sincerely,
                              Mary Brent
                              Director of Volunteers.

So she was "in"—but only on probation! The
word tempered Bonnie's excitement. Just what
did that mean? On what did her full acceptance
depend?

"On how you take to it, of course!" Laura declared wisely when Bonnie shared the news
with the rest of the family. "I've read all about
it in books about nurses."

"But Bonnie isn't going into nursing!" Mrs.
Schuyler protested.

"Still, she has to know something about taking
care of sick people," Laura declared. "You can
practice on me, Bon. Shall I get into bed and
let you do things to me, so you'll be that much
ahead of the other girls?"

"It wouldn't do much good at this point,"
Bonnie replied, smiling. "I wouldn't know
where to begin. Besides, as I told you before,
Candy Stripers do not do things *to* people; only
for them."

Laura was disappointed. "Well, I'm going to
be a Candy Striper, too. I wish I knew how to
hurry and get to be fourteen. That's how old

you have to be before they'll take you at Hamilton, isn't it?"

"Yes," Bonnie called over her shoulder as she scooted out the back door to tell Nancy of her acceptance.

She was twenty minutes early on Saturday morning, but already the spacious, pale blue Meeting Room was filling up with chattering girls. Bonnie paused in the doorway, suddenly wishing that Anne were there to go into this with her. She was still not used to doing things by herself. But then she recognized half a dozen girls from her own school and moved toward them through a crowd of strangers. The Medical Center served a wide area, so there were girls from nearby towns, also.

Bonnie was surprised to see Mavis Watts from her high school. Mavis was a rather sultry brunette, who always made her think of Carmen—on the prowl, and she had a justly deserved "man chaser" reputation. Near her was a complete contrast, shy little Carol Kent, with her arms held close to her sides and her hands clasped tight.

Denise Chapman, who usually had to have things explained to her three or four times and maybe written down in words of one syllable, came hurrying in with Pixie Chase. Pixie's per-

petually surprised expression was more pro-
nounced than usual.

"Hi!" she panted, thumping her thin chest.
"Guess what? I got lost. My Indian Scout Great-
Granduncle Zeke would be ashamed of me and
that's for true. I came in through something
called the Out Patients' Department and wound
up in the kitchen!"

Ginny Lou Elkin joined the group. "Was
there anything yummy to eat?" she asked in a
warm, slurry drawl.

"I didn't wait long enough to find out,
Sugar." Pixie gave a perfect imitation of
Ginny's voice. "And you shouldn't be thinking
about food." She poked a finger into Ginny's
soft round arm. "Didn't you tell me you were
going on a diet?"

"I'm going." Ginny sighed. "Tomorrow. And
you don't need to sound so superior about it,
Pixie Chase. I've seen you eat, but with your
metabolism, or however you stay so skinny, you
don't have to find out how hard it is to give up
food." She looked famished at the mere thought
and the other girls laughed sympathetically and
linked arms with her.

"Listen, you interrupted my very fascinating
experiences on the way here," Pixie grumbled.
"I ducked up the stairs and came out on the

second floor—and there was this *man*—in a bathrobe!"

"So what?" Denise asked.

"Well-ll, I've never seen a strange man in a bathrobe before!"

"This is a hospital, you're going to see a lot of strange men," Mavis told her and moved on.

Pixie's eyes opened wide. "That's right, isn't it? But I've never been in a hospital before, and I've never seen a man in bed before, except my father."

"Neither have I," Bonnie confessed. "I really don't know anything about sick people."

"I guess we'll all learn," Ginny Lou drawled. "That's what we're here for."

"Imagine! Me following in the footsteps of Florence Nightingale, Edith Cavell and *Sue Barton!*" Pixie burbled. "My mother can't believe that I have such worthwhile impulses. She hopes the experience here will settle me down."

"I doubt it," Denise said. "But speaking of settling, how about those chairs over there, near the front, so we can hear everything."

The girls slipped into a row and smoothed their skirts. Pixie was soon off again. "How Dense, here, is going to get everything through her thick little skull is beyond me," she said impudently.

"I'll write everything down," Denise told her,

and produced a notebook. "I shall be a model
Candy Striper. Mrs. Brent will point to me
with pride."

"That'll be the day." Pixie chuckled.

"It'll be the day if she points to you with
pride," Bonnie said, "if you carry on like this
all the time. Hush up, now. There's Mrs. Brent,
stepping up on the platform."

Behind the platform was a blackboard and a
rolled up projection screen. Nearby stood X-
ray picture racks and a television set. This
room was frequently used by doctors and interns for lectures and discussions. Mrs. Brent
moved to the lectern and faced the assembled
girls. Every seat was filled. Bonnie wondered
if the Center would be able to use them all.

Mrs. Brent, very trim in a summer weight
navy blue suit, her abundant hair confined in
a shiny chignon, tapped the edge of the lectern
with a pencil. "Good morning, girls!" The
room quieted. "May I again welcome you to the
ranks of Candy Stripers, our youngest, but already proved, volunteer service. Before the end
of this meeting you will be issued the official
Candy Striper's uniform, and then you will
look like this!"

She beckoned and two pinafored girls swished
up to stand on either side of her. Each had an
array of blue stars across the front of her

pinafore bib and an enameled pin, "Issued after five hundred hours of service!" Mrs. Brent said.

As Bonnie eyed the Candy Stripers with awe, she thought they swelled with pride at Mrs. Brent's words.

"This uniform, a pinafore with a sleeved white blouse, soft-soled shoes—white preferably —and neat, not bulky white socks, identifies teen-age volunteers everywhere," Mrs. Brent continued. "Many hospitals throughout the country now have girls like yourselves serving them, although the ages at which girls are admitted into the ranks vary from fourteen to sixteen, or even eighteen. We are very proud of *our* Candy Stripers and we expect all the girls who join them to uphold that pride."

"Oh, my!" Behind her, Bonnie heard Mavis stifle a yawn.

"When you are in uniform we expect you to behave with dignity. No running, no loud talking or laughing, no gum chewing, please. And no munching on the floors at any time. If your hours here take you through lunch or dinner time, that meal will be provided for you in the staff cafeteria. When you come here after school, cookies and milk will be served You are girls on whom we depend, and so we shall see to it that you are well nourished."

A laugh rippled over her audience.

"I'm too well nourished now," Ginny Lou murmured audibly, amid giggles.

"We'll help you take care of that, too," Mrs. Brent promised, smiling. "You come see me some afternoon and we'll go over your diet." She became quite serious. "Hospitals need volunteers these days, and believe me, we appreciate every hour that is given to us by our people whether they are fourteen or forty. The thing we want to impress upon you is this: When you are here and in uniform, you will be treated as mature persons worthy of trust and respect."

Pixie Chase distracted Bonnie's attention by giving a smug "so there!" nod.

"Never discuss anything you see or hear in the hospital with outsiders," Mrs. Brent cautioned. "This verse might help you remember:

> WHAT YOU SEE HERE,
> WHAT YOU HEAR HERE,
> WHEN YOU LEAVE HERE,
> LET IT STAY HERE!"

She was silent for a moment, allowing her words to sink in. Then she said, "Before you are a full-fledged Candy Striper and are given the hospital insignia to wear on the front of your pinafore, you will have twenty hours of classwork plus assignments in various departments where you will work with a senior Candy Striper. When you have completed these, you will leave the ranks of probationers and start recording your hours for the first blue star, given at the end of one hundred hours. Five such stars will entitle you to a pin. At the end of two years, at a special ceremony, you will be given a cap to wear."

Nancy had mentioned that, Bonnie recalled. She supposed that in a way it would bring Nancy a step closer to her goal of being a nurse. But, of course, it was nothing she had in her own plans. She didn't think she'd like real nursing.

"I hope," Mrs. Brent went on, "that most of you will stay with us for two years and more. We have a winter schedule adjusted to your school hours. We hope that some of you will come back as paid assistants during your college summers and that later on, as you marry, have children and watch them go off to school, you will join the ranks of the Pink Ladies—the adult volunteers. At no time in your life is there a period when your community hospital will not have need of your services.

"It is an honor to be allowed to work here," she said, her head high "I hope all of you will pass through your 'probie' period with flying colors. And now I will turn you over to Mrs. Ruth Collins, R.N., who is charged with our in-service training. She will put you through your orientation course and will introduce you to some hospital procedures now. Then we shall all have lunch here, buffet style, and after that your uniforms will be issued."

"Oh, boy!" Denise bounced in her chair as Mrs. Brent stepped down.

But Pixie stared at Bonnie, frowning. "Golly," she said. "How do you feel about all this?"

Bonnie shrugged. "Solemn. I feel as if I'm about to take the veil."

"No. The Lamp," Pixie said. "You know, Florence Nightingale, the Lady with the Lamp. But maybe Candy Stripers rate only a candle."

"From that talk I'd say we rated a match." Mavis leaned toward the trio. "I'm not sure I'm worthy of all this honor. But," she looked bored, "I haven't anything better to do with my summer."

Bonnie was about to snap that this was no attitude to take, when she remembered that her own motives for joining the Candy Stripers had not been too lofty either!

Mrs. Collins, tall and imposing, like Juno in a white uniform, the cap on her upswept graying hair almost like a crown, stepped to the platform and rapped for attention.

She surveyed the group and her blue eyes twinkled. "Without a doubt," she said, "you are the healthiest and loveliest group of girls I have ever seen! And that is one of the reasons why Candy Stripers are so welcome in hospitals. We expect patients to get well just looking at you."

The girls glanced at each other and smiled self-consciously.

"On our side," she went on, "we offer you what we believe will be valuable experience, no matter what you decide to do later in life. Those of you who plan careers in medical fields will have ample opportunities to observe doctors, nurses and technicians at work, to crystallize your own ideas toward those fields. Every one of you will profit from contact with many kinds of people in all sorts of conditions and walks of life. Knowing how to get along with people is a valuable asset.

"This afternoon you will have an orientation tour. You will be taken through the five floors and the basement. You will see that in the great Y-shape of this institution all the floors are laid out in exactly the same manner. This makes it easier to find one's way about. For example, utility rooms are in exactly the same place on each floor. Stretcher rooms have the same location. Wheel chairs can be found there, too, and certain other equipment, like IV poles, which are not for growing ivy, by the way, but are metal stands for supporting equipment used in intravenous injections."

The girls giggled and she smiled pleasantly.

"The Nurse's Station is located in exactly the same place on every floor, and from that post, with the aid of mirrors, those in charge can see everything that goes on on the floor."

She outlined a number of other details, and then glancing at her watch, announced that it was lunchtime. Almost at once the kitchen staff appeared with two Monel metal carts, and in a twinkling a buffet was spread before the new Candy Stripers.

"I'm starved," Bonnie said. "I had no idea listening could make one so hungry."

"Come along then, before you faint dead away and we have to carry you." Pixie grabbed one arm and Ginny the other, and together they propelled Bonnie forward.

"I can hardly wait to get into my uniform," the one-tracked Denise said as the girls found places to sit once more, paper plates laden with sandwiches and cookies and small cartons of milk. "What is it that makes a uniform so devastating? When my brother came home on leave in his Air Force blues all the girls practically swooned, me included. His own sister!"

"You don't expect all the girls to swoon over *your* uniform, do you?" Pixie teased.

"No, silly. Only the boys."

"And when do you expect the boys to see you? You're not planning to wear it to school, are you?"

"Of course not. But boys get sick, too, don't they? Some of them are bound to wind up here —and then they'll see me!" Denise finished triumphantly.

"You and all the rest of us." Bonnie quashed her jubilation. "Every last ray of sunshine among us!"

"Oh-h, *vinegar!*" Denise made a face. "You've practically spoiled my appetite." She took a fierce bite on her sandwich.

"Nothing ever spoils mine," Ginny Lou mourned.

The uniforms were distributed when the girls were finished eating. Bonnie's size twelve fitted her perfectly. Ginny Lou tried desperately to squeeze into a size sixteen, but it was hopeless.

"I'm sorry, Ginny. I'm afraid you'll have to make your own," Mrs. Brent said. "I'll give you the pattern and the cloth."

"All right." Ginny Lou's smile was unsteady, and Bonnie felt sorry for her.

"Diet!" Pixie told her callously. "Resolve right now. Why, I had an aunt who lost one hundred and eleven pounds once!"

"Oh-h, shut up," the gentle Ginny snapped. "Or—or I'll sit on you!"

Armed with her crisp new pinafore, Bonnie moved away from a noisy group to read the Junior Aides Volunteer Pledge:

Believing that the Hamilton Medical Center has a real need of my services as a Striper—

I will be punctual and conscientious in the fulfillment of my duties and accept supervision graciously.

I will conduct myself with dignity, courtesy and consideration.

I will consider as confidential all information which I may hear directly or indirectly concerning a patient, doctor, or nurse; and will seek no information about any patient.

I will take any problems, criticism or suggestions to the Director of Volunteers.

I will endeavor to make my work professional in quality.

I will uphold the traditions and standards of the Junior Aides at all times.

There was room for her signature, address and telephone number. Bonnie felt a wave of uneasiness at the formality of the pledge. Her original excitement had ebbed and she wondered if she was getting into something deeper than she had intended.

She reread the pledge again. This was not play-acting. This was real and earnest, with a sound of no nonsense about it. The wearing of the pink candy-striped uniform would signify her acceptance of all the rules and duties she had been hearing about. Did she want to spend her summer so hedged in with rules and duties?

"How soulful we look," Mavis said at her elbow, misunderstanding Bonnie's preoccupation. "I guess the tour comes next. I wonder if they'll take us into the morgue?"

Bonnie started. Mavis liked to shock people. Bonnie gave her a cool stare. "Why?" she asked. "Won't you go?"

The other girl shrugged superciliously.

Before she could answer, Ginny Lou came up. "I wonder if they'll let us see the babies?" she asked. "I'd love to have a brand-new baby in my arms, wouldn't you?"

Bonnie turned her back on Mavis. What an unpleasant girl. She smiled at Ginny. "I guess they'll let us see them—but I doubt very much

that they'll let us hold them. Aren't they awfully delicate?"

"Not really." This was Carol, her pale, shy
face almost pink with excitement. "At least,
that's what I've read in magazines. When we're
trained we can work in Pediatrics, and there
we'll be allowed to hold tiny tots to feed and
comfort, but only trained nurses handle the
newborn. My cousin is a nurse here. She told
me."

"I'm going to ask for Pediatrics duty," Ginny
Lou announced. "I love little children."

"They're always crying." Mavis made a face.
"I wouldn't take Pediatrics for anything. I'm
going to ask for Floor Duty. That will be a lot
more interesting."

Bonnie looked beyond her and saw a group of
uniformed Candy Stripers approaching. They
were senior girls, bedecked with blue service
stars. Nancy Wheeler was among them.

Mrs. Brent clapped her hands for silence, divided the new girls into groups of ten for the
hospital tour and assigned a senior to each
group. Bonnie was pleased to find herself in
Nancy's charge. Pixie, Denise, and unfortunate-
ly Mavis, were there, also.

four

THE HOSPITAL WAS ENORMOUS, AND ALTHOUGH
Nancy was a good guide, it wasn't long before
Bonnie was thoroughly confused and "lost."
Quiet rooms, treatment rooms, solariums, diet
kitchens seemed to flash by her. They spent a
little more time in the Pediatrics Wing, shut
off from the rest of the floor by large heavy
doors. The small patients were in beds and
cribs behind glass walls, so that they could be
observed easily by passing nurses.

Some of the children were heartbreakingly
quiet, others wailed unceasingly, and one boy,
obviously ready to go home, entertained the

45

visitors by standing on his head inside the high sides of his bed. The crying children bothered Bonnie. She did not think she would be able to stand working in Pediatrics. She was afraid she would start crying with them. They seemed so small and helpless. She wondered what Ginny Lou's reaction would be after seeing this section, but her friend's motherly spirit was undaunted. She still wanted Pediatrics duty.

The maternity patients on the third floor wore gay bed jackets and were surrounded by flowers. They smiled at the new girls.

"Everybody is usually healthy and happy here," Nancy confided. "There isn't ever too much to do on this floor, except in Central Supply, which is over in the north wing. All used equipment is brought here to be sterilized and repackaged. See, there's a Candy Striper checking a surgeon's gown, and that one is making drainage pads." She signaled for the group to move on. "Sterile supplies are requisitioned at this window."

Before they passed on, Bonnie was able to read the sign tacked to the wall on the right, over a bell button:

> In God we trust
> But here in CSR
> *Everyone* must have a requisition.

This means YOU!
Please ring bell. Once.

She wasn't sure what all that meant but was glad to see that even in hospital parlance there was room for humor.

Further passage down this corridor was blocked by opaque half-glass doors. A sign here read: *Delivery Room.*

"What's that?" one of the girls asked.

Before Nancy could reply, Mavis broke in with exaggerated sweetness, "That, darling, is where babies come from. That's where the stork leaves them."

The girl who had asked the question turned scarlet, but Nancy ignored the interruption and the sarcasm, saying calmly:

"We have every known device to insure the safety of mothers and infants here. Once we delivered a premature seventeen-ounce baby girl, and recently she celebrated her second birthday! She was one of the smallest such babies ever to survive." Nancy said it with as much pride as if she'd helped in the delivery and care of the tiny mite herself. "We delivered triplets last week," she added.

"Oo-ooh!" The girls seemed charmed by the idea.

"Are the nurseries back there, too?" Bonnie

asked, eying the forbidding doors regretfully.
There was something mysterious and wonderful about the newborn and she wanted to see
them.

"No, the babies are in the East Wing. I'll take
you there next."

There were several nurseries set up behind
protecting glass walls. The babies were incredibly tiny in their bassinets, each one wrapped
in either a pink or a blue blanket. Gowned and
masked nurses moved among them attentively.
Nancy had difficulty in budging her charges
from this fascinating sight.

Finally, however, she succeeded in getting
them down the stairs to the second floor. "All
the patients on this floor have had operations
of one kind or another." She indicated the east
and west wings on either side of the nurse's station. "The OR is in the north wing," she waved
toward the closed doors. "That's the operating
section. We never go in there, except to deliver
messages at the nurse's station, or on special
assignment to help clean instruments."

"Oh, no!" One of the more delicate girls
wailed softly.

"Don't worry," Nancy reassured. "You won't
be sent to do that except on your own request,
after Mrs. Brent is very sure of you. The same
applies to duty in the Clinic. Anyway, during

the summer the Candy Stripers don't work in OR at all because then we have college fellows in there."

"*Boys?*" The girls squealed, forgetting hospital decorum for the moment.

"Yes. Real boys." Nancy laughed. "They're pre-med students, eager to get hospital background. They'll do anything—clean-up, orderly, lab work."

Mavis' large bold eyes glittered. "I knew that," she said.

"Yes? Well, come along. Down to the first floor we go. . . . This is the main lobby. Most of you came in through here, so you've seen it. The East Wing is very important to you, because that is where the central laboratory is, as well as the blood bank, pathology department, X-ray and so on. This is where many of your errands will lead you. In your other orientation courses you will learn all about this section."

"I'll never find my way around this place," Denise wailed. "Never, never. I'll have to have a guide with me every minute."

Nancy heard her and spoke comfortingly. "And so you will, until you do know your way around. That is why you have the orientation course."

"Look! A chapel!" Pixie said suddenly. "How sweet. May we stop a minute?"

"Of course. It's nonsectarian, and every Sunday afternoon ministers from different churches hold services here."

The girls crowded inside. Two rows of pews led down to a marble altar. Above it glowed a handsome stained glass window, showing the Savior, and on either side of this were smaller windows. A doctor was shown in one, and a nurse with a baby in the other. Bonnie liked the symbolic use of the figures and felt strangely moved by their significance here.

The girls filed out again quietly.

"The coffee and gift shops are here," Nancy said, "and some of our most faithful Volunteers work there. Both shops are self-supporting, and all profits are used for gifts to the hospital. Incidentally, remember that professional people —and that goes for volunteers too—do not accept tips. If someone offers you a tip, explain that you appreciate the thought but cannot accept it. However, if he wishes to express thanks for service, there is a special thank-you fund for future building. You can even offer to put the money in the collection box if the patient wants you to."

"Building fund?" Bonnie was astonished. "But this place is brand new!"

"Yes, and already we need more space. You have no idea how many people are using hospital service nowadays. Our community has grown, and health insurance plans make it possible for more people to have this kind of medical care."

Nancy let the girls mull that over, before pointing out the staff dining room at the end of the corridor, and then backtracked to a closed door. "Oh. Something must be going on in there," she said, "but this is where your future classes will be held. We do not have a nursing school here. However, the Hamilton Medical Center is affiliated with a number of nursing colleges where the girls get their Bachelor of Science degree along with the R.N. You practically have to be a B.S., R.N. now to get into any important administrative posts," she explained. "Well, for hospital experience these colleges send their students here, and this is their classroom, as well as a lecture room for our new volunteers, and our paid workers who need training.

"You'll remember where it is, won't you? If not, you can ask at the Information Desk when you come in." She looked at Denise whose brow was furrowed with concentration, and Dense seemed relieved by the suggestion.

On the ground floor Nancy pointed out the

contagion wing, called the Hartwell Pavilion. "It's practically empty at the moment," she said, sounding pleased. "No one outside the special nursing staff is allowed in there, but this wing has an outside terrace all along the rooms, from which patients can be visited through screened windows. Down there," she pointed north, "is the Physical Medicine department. Some of you will be stationed there, or will be asked to bring patients down for treatments. Beyond is the Dietician's Office and the kitchen. And here," Bonnie thought Nancy stood a bit straighter as she said it, "is where I work, the OPD—Clinic, or Out Patient Department. People who cannot afford to pay private doctors come here for treatments. Here also come emergency cases." She did not go into details, but noting that the girls were growing tired, led them on the last stage of the tour.

"The basement," she announced.

This area was rather dreary, with none of the grace notes of the upper floors where patients were treated.

"All sorts of necessary things are located here, like the laundry. Have you any idea of the mountains of linen used by the hospital? Take a look at those carts!"

"*Yikes!*" Pixie made a comic face. "I'm glad I didn't volunteer to wash all that!"

The girls laughed.

"Storage rooms, the mail room," Nancy pointed them out in quick succession. "Sacks of mail come in every day and Pink Ladies and Candy Stripers do the sorting and delivering. The autopsy room is here, too, and the morgue."

Her words fell into a chilly pool of silence.

"Do any of you want to see those?"

"I'm game," Pixie declared.

"All right." Nancy opened the door. Bonnie and three other girls crowded in behind her. The rest stayed in the hall, curious but hesitant.

"This is a very necessary part of the hospital," Nancy said gently. "Here doctors learn a great deal about diseases."

The autopsy room was very utilitarian, Bonnie thought. There was a metal operating table, filing cabinets and many shelves filled with a mysterious array of jars. She did not want to inspect these too closely. A peculiar odor seemed to permeate the place.

"Formaldehyde," Nancy said. "It's a preservative."

"Like in the biology room in school," Bonnie whispered. "For frogs and things."

"Ugh! Such canned goods!" Pixie, whose curiosity had overcome her, backed out fast.

and the other girls followed, not at all loathe to retreat.

The morgue was unspectacular. "Nothing like in the movies," Pixie complained. "Just a couple of lockers, like old iceboxes."

"What did you expect? Marble slabs? Sheeted figures?" Mavis asked. She glanced at Nancy. "I guess we've seen it all, from the cradle to the grave."

Nancy's usually serene forehead puckered. She seemed to be puzzled by Mavis' offhand manner. "I guess you have," she agreed. "I'll take you back to the lobby. I hope you have enjoyed your tour."

A round-robin murmur of thank-you's winged among the girls.

In the elevator Nancy said, "You can mark down three hours on your orientation course in Mrs. Brent's book. Next week you will have two hours of instruction and two hours of duty with a senior Candy Striper."

"You mean we'll really get out and *work?*" Pixie asked ecstatically. "*Do things to people?*"

"*For* people," Nancy emphasized. "And under strict supervision. No ministering angels running wild.

Bonnie left the Medical Center in a daze. It had been a great deal to take in at one time, this glimpse into a hospital world. But the other girls chattered around her, apparently able to shed the experience as soon as they were out of doors. They all lived either in town or in the opposite direction from hers, so Bonnie said good-by and dashed for her bus, pony tail flying. The run increased her circulation and served also to clear her head. Confusion was gradually replaced by more orderly thinking.

The hospital was quite a place, and it held a promise of many interesting experiences. As she thought about it and her impressions began to fall into line, she kept hearing the animated voices of Mrs. Brent, the Junoesque Mrs. Collins, and Nancy's unqualified enthusiasm for the Center and all it held. A curious zeal to be a part of it all began to seep back into her. She began to want a closer look at the various departments they had gone through so quickly during the tour. But a whole week would go by before she was due to return for her training class. Why couldn't they have set up the schedule more closely!

As she got off the bus in front of her house, Bonnie saw a familiar jumble of small boy arms and legs wrapped around a larger brown form, prone on the Schuyler front lawn.

Rock Caldwell was at the bottom of the heap.

five

THE LITTLE BOYS SWARMING OVER ROCK WERE
Nancy Wheeler's brothers, Chris and Chubb.

"Well!" Bonnie said loudly as she stood over
them.

There was an instant upheaval and Rock
scrambled to his feet, a blond giant with tumbled hair, a frown knitting his brows.

"Where've you been all day?" he demanded,
unmindful of the boys' howls of protest.
"What's this Laura tells me about you playing
nurse at the Medical Center?"

"I'm not playing!" Bonnie bristled.

"Okay, don't get mad." Rock turned to the

boys. "Beat it, kids," he growled. "I'll show you how to tackle next time."

Chris and Chubb gave Bonnie a disgusted look and tramped away.

"What I want to know," Rock said, arms akimbo, "is did we or did we not to have a date to go bicycling today?"

Bonnie's hand flew to her mouth. Rock's bike was lying accusingly on its side near the drive. "I forgot!" she wailed. "I completely forgot. I've been up in the air all week——"

"Yeah? Over whom?" He scowled suspiciously.

"Oh hush. Over being a Candy Striper at the hospital."

"Why? What do you want to hang around the hospital for?"

"Well, for one thing, I want to do something useful this summer. Remember, *I'm* not going away—as you are." Bonnie angled toward the back yard and plumped herself into the hammock, holding her uniform tenderly, so as not to rumple its freshness.

Rock sank on the grass beside her and began to chew a blade. "I wish I hadn't taken this counselor job. But the money will be free and clear at the end of the summer, with my board and keep all taken care of—and no place to spend it up in the mountains. I have my eye on the sweetest little convertible a guy's going to be ready to sell come September. Boy, oh boy, I'll be able to take us around in style then."

She smiled and reached out to pat his hand.

"Will you miss me?" he asked.

Her answer was lost in a roll of drumbeats and a clash of cymbals.

Rock glanced toward the Coburn house. "Our date for the dance still stands, doesn't it?"

"Of course! The Hamilton Swing Band is going to play, isn't it?"

"Yeah." Rock listened to the rhythmic drumbeats thoughtfully. "I never realized before how close you're living to that new guy. And I heard him say the other day he's got a swell job lined up, so he's going to be around all summer, too. How well do you know him?"

"Whom? Cliff Coburn?" Bonnie wanted to laugh. This exhibition of jealousy was rather fun, even though unfounded.

"Yeah—?" Rock leaned over demandingly.

"Well-ll, we're neighbors, of course. Hello. Good-by. That sort of thing." Bonnie was too honest to yield to the temptation to embroider.

"Huh. Be sure you keep it that way. And don't go falling for any of those interns at the Center."

"Rock! They're men. It takes forever to get

through medical school. By the time they get here——"

"Yeah. I know. They have long gray beards. Bonnie," his voice grew husky, "I want you for my steady. To be sure of you."

Bonnie's arms tightened around the pink-striped uniform. Rock's voice thrilled her. She sat up and looked deep into his troubled blue eyes, at the little hump where he'd had his nose broken in a football skirmish, at the cap over his front tooth, a casualty of the same cause. Rock was a darling. No intellectual giant; he barely managed to skin by on his grades. But he was awfully good looking and sweet, and at this moment she was almost sure she was in love with him. Not forever, of course. But for now.

"Oh, Rock," she said gently. "I want to be your steady. But Mother——" Even as she said it, Bonnie wondered if she really meant it. For all the dating security the term implied, as her parents had pointed out, this was the time to meet lots of people, get to know all kinds. "Otherwise," Mother had said, and quite reasonably, "how will you know what sort of person is the right one for you, if you narrow and limit your friendships to a 'steady.'"

"Does your mother have to know?" Rock asked. "I could give you my ring and you could wear it inside your—the way some girls do."

Bonnie shook her head. "I don't do things that way. If I'm your steady, I want to be proud of it—let everybody know."

"Yeah." Rock rested his square chin on a big hand propped against his knees. "I guess I'd rather have it that way, too. Okay. We'll play it your way. Movies tonight?"

She nodded.

He got up, tipped her chin and stared down at her. "You're cute," he said. She knew Rock wanted to kiss her, but he didn't. Instead, he tweaked her pony tail. "I gotta blow. See you later."

He went off, and she remained in the hammock, thinking dreamily about him. Appropriately Cliff Coburn's drumbeats became soft flicks and then mere whisks as he changed to brushes.

The sound stopped. Bonnie rocked gently. She heard a rustle and a faint metallic bang nearby and sat up. Cliff was in his back yard, emptying a wastebasket into the incinerator. He was tall and rangy, his black hair trained into a kind of stand-up crewcut. Not handsome. His mouth was a bit large. He was not gorgeously muscled like Rock, and yet, when he moved, Cliff seemed to have springs in his feet. And his mind—she'd heard of his prowess in classes. He was lightning quick, the kids said.

As she watched, Cliff dug out a small book from his back pocket and proceeded to read, casting an occasional glance at the flames licking out of the wire incinerator. This boy never let a moment go to waste. He intrigued her. Was that because he was always busy, always on the go? Or because he never reacted to her, the way other boys did, with a quick appraising interest? She'd make him look over now, no matter how absorbed he was in his book.

"Hi!" she called.

It surprised Cliff. "Oh. Hi. I didn't know you were over there. Hope this smoke doesn't bother you."

That was the most he'd ever said to her! "Not at all," Bonnie told him, resisting the impulse to wave off the billows floating in her direction. She left the Hammock and came closer to the low hedge separating the properties. Rock would have leaped over it and been at her side in an instant. Not Cliff. He stood right there, on guard beside his old incinerator, and even glanced back at his book!

Bonnie felt her face warming, but she wouldn't give up. "You're playing at the dance next week?" she asked.

"Yes." She thought that was the end of it, but then he added, "I suppose you're going."

She nodded. "I go to most of the dances—"

She was going to add how much she enjoyed his rhythmic drums, but the way he looked her up and down stopped her. His eyes were cool.

"It follows," he said, and it didn't sound like a compliment! It was more like a criticism. As if there were something wrong in being reasonably popular and enjoying dances. "Excuse me," he said, "I have to go." The fire was out and there was no further need for him to be in the yard!

Bonnie's mouth opened and color flared in her cheeks, but Cliff was already halfway to the house. If a stone had been handy she would have heaved it after him. Of all the nerve. Who did he think he was! Frustrated expletives frothed in her mind.

"Hey, Bonnie!"

Her sister's voice, coming from the porch, checked her anger. Why on earth was she getting into such an uproar over Cliff Coburn! Especially when she had Rock Caldwell at her beck and call—at least until the day after school was out.

"For goodness sakes! What's the matter with you?" Laura grabbed her sister's arm and shook it. "I've been calling and calling to you! What happened at the Center? Aren't you going to tell us all about it? Mother's waiting to hear, too. Oh, Bon! You got your uni-

form! Will you let me try it on? And look what
I found in the back of my bookcase!" Expecting no answers to her barrage, Laura waved a
booklet in front of Bonnie's nose.

"What is it?" Bonnie asked, impatiently
breaking away from her sister's hold.

"It's the booklet they put out when the Medical Center first opened. It tells about it and it
shows floor plans of every single floor in the
place! Isn't that wonderful?"

"Wonderful," Bonnie agreed dispassionately.

"How can you be such a dope?" Laura asked
with sisterly candor. "You can study this and
know where everything is located. Then if you
have to go anyplace, you won't have to ask.
You'll know!"

For the first time Bonnie's attention was
caught. That's the way Laura worked. She was
always looking things up—in books, in pamphlets—she had mountains of those. She had an
amazing fund of information on the most un-
likely subjects and was more than willing to
share it with anyone who would listen. This
time, however, Laura really had something of
value for her. Bonnie forgot her irritation with
Cliff and moved toward the house with Laura,
studying the pamphlet along the way. As she ex-
amined the floor plans, details of her tour of
the building came to her clearly. This was a

good thing to have, and when she went to the Center she would not feel hopelessly lost on the floors.

"Thanks, Laura," she said, in a burst of appreciation for her young sister's thoughtfulness. "Where is Mom? Wait till you both hear about the tour they took us on. All over the hospital." Bonnie made a mental note to emphasize how neat and orderly and antiseptic everything was and how nice all the people seemed to be. She decided to delete some of the details of the visit to the basement, and the effect on her of the wailing youngsters in Pediatrics.

Both Mother and Laura listened to her account with great interest. Afterward, when Bonnie went upstairs, her younger sister cornered her. "I thought you said they took you *all* over," she said.

"They did."

"What about the basement?"

"I told you about the heaps of laundry."

"Oh, laundry!" Laura waved that away impatiently. She reached over to Bonnie's desk and picked up the booklet she had given her and riffled through the pages. "What about the morgue and the autopsy room?" she asked, pointing them out on the floor plans.

"Honestly, Laura, how morbid can you get?

That sort of thing has nothing to do with Candy Stripers," Bonnie parried.

"I suppose not," Laura agreed reluctantly. "But I'd want to see everything. And I want to know everything. You will tell me everything that happens, won't you? Promise?"

"Oh, yes. I promise," Bonnie said, laughing. "You're more persistent than a fly."

The comparison didn't bother Laura. "I can hardly wait till I can go to the Medical Center, too," she said, stroking Bonnie's new uniform. "Lucky, lucky you."

Bonnie shook her head as she began to pick up the avalanche of pamphlets dislodged in Laura's search for the hospital booklet. Whatever else her sister might be, she was certainly not orderly when it came to her belongings.

On the following Saturday the Medical Center appeared much less forbidding. Thanks to the floor plans, Bonnie found the Lecture Room and walked unerringly into a crowd of her fellow "probies."

Pixie spotted her at once and flew to her. "Look at this place!" she burbled. "It's a real nurses' classroom. I came early and I've explored everything—except the cabinets—and they're locked. See, here are the beds, just like in the rooms, and dressers and bed tables and everything. And look at Otis. Isn't he divine?"

Bonnie glanced over her shoulder, but saw no male figure.

"*There*, silly!" Pixie spun her around to come face to face with a skeleton, poised airily on a stand inside a glass case.

A small scream escaped despite Bonnie's effort to stifle it. "Pixie Chase, you wretch. You shouldn't do things like this to people," she scolded. "Besides, how do you know that's Otis?"

"Looks just like him," Pixie declared. "My fifth cousin, twice removed. Wouldn't eat a thing. They told him this would happen."

"You clown."

"And this," Pixie went on blandly, enjoying her role of guide, "is dear old Uncle Horace." She paused before a painted plaster anatomical figure with removable sections which displayed the human organs and muscles. "So generous," she said. "He'd give the shirt off his back. This time I guess he went too far."

"I'll say." Bonnie gave the torso her unenthusiastic attention. Did nurses have to know this much about the insides of people?

"Come meet some other members of my family," Pixie urged, dragging Bonnie over to a row of hospital beds occupied by life-size rubber dolls. "You don't believe me, eh? Well, read what it says on the name cards at the foot of each bed!"

Bonnie peered down and had to laugh. The lady doll was "Marilyn Chase." In another bed was a gentleman, presumably her husband, for he was named, "George Chase." And in a crib with raised sides was a little boy, "Bobby Chase."

"That's my sickly aunt and her family," Pixie said sorrowfully. "They just never get out of the hospital."

"Are you at it again with a new victim?" Denise asked, joining the two girls. "Ever since this nut got in here and discovered all this," she waved around the room, "she's been claiming every last thing as a relative."

"Can I help it if I have a large family?" Pixie asked plaintively. "They are named 'Chase' aren't they? What other proof do you want?"

"Oh, Pixie, sit down and hush up. You make my ears ache," Bonnie said. "Here comes Mrs. Collins."

As the girls found places in a row of tiered lecture chairs, Ginny Lou arrived and puffed in next to Bonnie.

"Just this minute finished the last buttonhole on my uniform," she gasped, smoothing down the skirt. "They let me make it in the sewing room here. Thank goodness I didn't have to do the blouse, too. I *am* going to reduce. I really am. I look like three Candy Stripers tied in the middle."

Mrs. Collins, cool and poised in her long-sleeved uniform, rapped for attention. At this session she went over the general duties of the Candy Stripers, asking the girls to follow their manuals as she talked. She stressed medical ethics and the necessity for mature behavior and observance of hospital rules.

"An infraction of the house rules means dismissal," she said. "We want only trustworthy, levelheaded people at the Center. Something that might be smiled at or passed off with a scolding elsewhere will not be tolerated here. The business of caring for the sick is too serious." With this unveiled warning, she went on, explaining hospital routine.

"Morning is the busiest time in the hospital," she said. "Baths and breakfast will be over before any of you come on duty. At eleven-thirty lunch is served to the patients, and incidentally, that is what some of you will help with today, with a senior Candy Striper to guide you.

"Let me show you how to prepare a patient for mealtime. The seats here are arranged so that all of you can see what I am doing from where you are." She moved briskly to one of the demonstration beds.

"Ready for lunch, Mrs. Chase?" she asked conversationally, treating the rubber doll in the bed like a real person.

Several of the girls tittered.

Mrs. Collins turned, and smiled with good humor. "I'll have you know," she said, "that the Chase family has given yeoman service to generations of students. We brought them with us from the old hospital. They are always treated like real patients."

Bonnie sent Pixie a mischievous glance. "But why are they called the 'Chase Family'?" she asked. "Why not Smith or Brown?"

"Because," Mrs. Collins explained, "these hospital dolls have been made by the Chase Company for many years, and always listed and sold by the supply houses as, 'Mrs. Chase,' 'Mr. Chase,' and 'Infant or Baby Chase.' The first names are tacked on by students, and changed from time to time, as different girls make up the worn-out name plates. The dolls are valuable to us because they are so pliable and at the same time durable for teaching modern techniques of bedside care."

Bonnie noticed that Pixie listened without the flicker of an eyelash.

Mrs. Collins went on. "At your next session you will learn how to make closed beds, open beds, and ether beds—for patients going to OR.

But right now I'll show you how to raise and lower patients—something you must not do, incidentally, before checking with the nurse, especially when the patient seems really ill, or has any tubes or other equipment around his bed."

The girls took this in solemnly, a sense of responsibility beginning to seep around them.

"As you see," Mrs. Collins said, stepping to one side, "there are two handles fitted into the foot of each bed. The left handle raises the head. The right handle raises the feet."

Bonnie saw Denise begin to write frantically in her notebook.

"Pull the handle out—so," Mrs. Collins demonstrated, "and turn it clockwise. To lower, turn counter clockwise—so. And remember, when you are through, push the handle back. Otherwise, sticking out like that, it can cause a fall, or a painful bruise on the legs.

"Now, to get back to Mrs. Chase and her lunch. Eating is very important and should be made as pleasant as possible for patients. They must be made comfortable, their hands washed, pillows plumped up.

"Sometimes you may be asked to feed a helpless patient, or a child." Mrs. Collins gave detailed instructions on this and then passed on to the answering of patients' signals on the floors, the arranging of bedside units, the passing of fresh water, and so on, demonstrating as she spoke.

At eleven Mrs. Brent came in with a group of senior girls and divided the new girls among them.

"I hope I don't fall flat on my face with a tray of food in my hands," Denise moaned. "Wouldn't that be awful?"

"But not insurmountable," Mrs. Brent laughed. "Come now, let's have a bit of positive thinking on this subject. You've all carried trays before, I'm sure. This is no different. And serving lunch, to which the patients usually look forward, will give you a chance to meet them face to face. Are we ready? Let's go, then."

Bonnie never quite knew how she got through the lunch period. She felt shy and dreadfully awkward, marching in with a tray, more or less in tandem with a senior girl, checking the name card on the tray with the name on the foot of the patient's bed. Mixing up trays was one of the sins to guard against. Placing the trays on the rolling bedside tables, trying to remember to carry them, so that when they were set down they would face the patient, kept her mind jumping nervously. She was so anxious to do her first job correctly that none of the patients registered with her as individuals.

In contrast, the senior girl chatted easily with the men and women she served, and the patients beamed at her. Bonnie thought they eyed her rather curiously, as if she were some misfit. She felt like one, too, although after the sixth or seventh tray she got the hang of it and found that she could walk into a room and smile.

The senior girls remained on the floors to help the kitchen staff clear the trays, but the newcomers returned to the classroom for sandwiches and milk and to discuss their experiences.

Pixie had served the surgical patients on Second and came down babbling away, full of confidence and details picked up by her sharp eyes. It seemed to take her no time at all to start talking like an old hand, Bonnie thought. Already she seemed to feel completely at home here.

But Denise returned to the classroom quite shaken. She had served the wrong tray to a diabetic who had been on the verge of eating when she had to dash in and snatch it away again. "It made me feel like a—a—such a meany," she finished, words failing her, "and the head nurse on the fourth floor just glared at me."

Ginny Lou was in a glow. She and Carol had been asked to feed a couple of young patients in Pediatrics. "They were darling. So eager to be loved and petted. I hated to leave them."

Bonnie glanced at Carol, who had a contented look on her face, as if she had found her place in life.

"I," said Mavis, her voice cool and slow in the excited chatter of the others, "managed to bump into the most romantic-looking intern on the fourth floor. That's where the very sick people are and he was making an emergency call. Dr. Dominic Ricci." She savored the name with pleasure, closing her eyes. "He could pass for a movie star. That old she-dragon of a nurse up there acted as if I'd done it on purpose. Well, I had!" Mavis laughed.

The other girls stared at her. A couple rushed over and Mavis had to describe the handsome intern in detail for them.

"How romantical." Pixie batted her eyes. "I can see what Mavis is going to have her mind on the rest of the summer."

"If she lasts that long," Nancy commented as she joined Bonnie's group. "Mrs. Collins is death on that sort of thing. How'd you kids make out?" she asked. When they told her, all in a rush, she smiled and added, "I'm to spend the rest of the time with you and help show you how to do things."

Mrs. Collins returned and classwork was resumed.

At home Bonnie again had to recount every single thing she'd learned, blow by blow, for Laura, who listened entranced. Her father appeared quite interested in the hospital work, too, and Bonnie wondered if there might not be a place for men volunteers at the Medical Center. She'd have to find out. As for Mother, she eyed Bonnie anxiously and kept cautioning her to wash her hands frequently. The soap, guaranteed to do away with twenty-seven germs, now appeared in the upstairs bathroom, too. Dear Mother, Bonnie thought, wishing she could dispel her worries in some way.

The orientation went on, week after week, each class period followed by duty in some area of the hospital. Bonnie learned how to make an unoccupied bed, with neat, mitered hospital corners; how to cover a stretcher and help transport a patient to X-ray, or for some special treatment—a task the girls were warned never to attempt alone. The stretchers rolled easily enough, but the wheels had a treacherous way of going off at tangents, hard for only one person to control.

Wheel chairs were folded up to take a minimum of storage space, and the girls learned to open these and to help patients into them. How to help admit a patient, how to help with the discharge of one, and information desk service, as well as delivery of mail, messages and flowers, were completed in class, and were followed by five hours of supervised duty in various hospital areas.

And then, with the Hamilton Medical Center Emblem sewn on the front of her uniform, Bonnie became a full-fledged Candy Striper!

School was over on Friday, and on Monday, June 24th, she would report for duty, all on her own, ready to start rolling up the hours toward her first blue star!

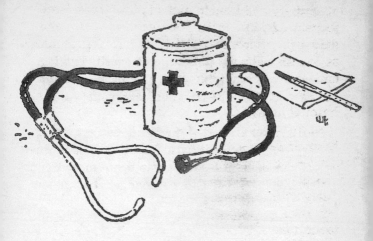

six

ANTICIPATING HER NEW STATUS AT THE MEDI-
cal center somehow eased the pangs of parting
from Rock Caldwell. He held her close on Saturday night and kissed her—hard—and then
was gone. Bonnie thought of the long summer
ahead, lonely and desolate, until she remem-
bored her work at the Center. Having had a
sample of it already, she knew it would keep her
busy—especially since she had signed up for five
full days a week. With Rock away, and Anne
gone, and their beach house rented, what else
was there to do?

When she reported for duty at Mrs. Brent's

office, Pixie, Denise and Mavis were already there, signing in in the big looseleaf Candy Striper's Record Book, lying on the counter beneath the name tag bulletin board. The tags, turned over and hung in the proper section, indicated at a glance where everyone on duty was stationed.

Mrs. Brent greeted the girls with a smile. "We seem very healthy in Hamilton this morning," she said. "Lots of people being discharged means lots of beds to be changed completely and made up. How about it, girls?"

"Oh, sure. We're willing," Pixie said, glancing at the others.

"Fine. If two of you work together on each bed, it will be easier and go faster." She reached for the telephone. "I'll tell Miss Winters, the supervisor on Fourth, that you're coming." When she hung up, she said, "Miss Winters is off the floor, but her assistant, Miss Kent, will tell you what to do."

The girls found their tags and set them up on the bulletin board in the Fourth Floor area. Then they rustled off for the elevator.

"Press the 'hold' button!" Denise said. "These doors move so fast, the other day the back of my pinafore almost got clipped because I wasn't quick enough!" She hopped inside like a rabbit and the others followed. The elevator whirred upward smoothly.

On Fourth a pretty blonde nurse stepped out of the semicircular desk area which partitioned the nurse's station from the rest of the floor. "I'm Miss Kent," she told the girls softly. "We're awfully glad to have you help out. Here is a list of rooms from which patients have been discharged." She handed the slip to Bonnie, who was trying hard not to stare. "The units have all been cleaned out, the beds stripped, the mattresses brushed, and the rubber sheets carbolized—sterilized, that is—by the floor attendants. All you have to do is make the beds up fresh." She glanced down the long halls. "The linen is being distributed now. If you get into any difficulties, come and tell me." She smiled dismissal, and the Candy Stripers moved off.

"Wow!" Pixie whispered. "That's what I call a goddess. Isn't she gorgeous!"

"M'mmm. Kent," Bonnie murmured. "Could she be Carol's cousin? Carol did say she had one working here."

"Could be," Denise agreed, "but there's certainly no resemblance, except maybe around the eyes?"

"Yes. They both have two," Mavis injected dryly, and swung into the first semiprivate room.

Bonnie had made beds before, both in class and on duty with a senior Candy Striper, and had even jotted down the procedure, step by step. The makings of a bed were very important to a hospital patient, she had learned, for the smallest fold in the wrong place could be most irritating to a sick person—or sheets that rode up and rumpled, or pulled out from the bottom.

"I don't mind bedmaking," Denise said, pairing herself with Pixie and thus leaving Bonnie with Mavis. "But it's these up and down levers that drive me crazy. I can never remember which is which or which way to turn the things."

"Well, gosh, here's an empty bed to practice on. Go ahead," Pixie invited, pushing the room door shut.

"All right. I will." Denise pulled out the handle at the foot of the empty bed. "Left—head up. Right—feet up." She wound and unwound energetically, and finally, carried away, put both the head and the foot part of the bed up simultaneously.

"Look out! You're squashing the patient!" Pixie giggled.

"I know!" Denise laughed, grinding away.

"Let's do it the other way!" Pixie suggested, suiting action to the word. Soon the pranksters had the bed humped in the middle. "The rack!" Pixie chortled. "Boy, what we could do to people we don't like!"

They all burst into hysterical laughing, and Bonnie thought uneasily what a story this would make for Laura.

"Put it down," she urged. "Put it down, girls."

"All right." Denise reached for the handle and turned. It seemed stuck. She grabbed the other one. That, too, refused to budge. "Golly! What do we do now?"

"What do you mean, 'we'?" Mavis asked. "That's a problem for you clowns."

Both Denise and Pixie tried frantically to turn the handles, but the bed remained in the same grotesque position.

"Do you suppose we've broken it?" Denise's voice trembled.

"I wouldn't be surprised." Mavis was no comfort. "And if you have, you must pay for the repairs. You know the rule. If you break any piece of equipment in a hospital you're responsible for its repair or replacement."

"But a bed!" Denise turned pale.

"Let me try," Bonnie volunteered. She strained at the handle and thought the foot section had begun to go down when the door opened and a shocked gasp stopped her.

"What is the meaning of this?" a harsh voice demanded.

The girls stood frozen.

Miss Emma Winters, the gray-haired fourth floor supervisor, marched into the room, flicked each girl with a shriveling glance and then pushed Bonnie away from the bed cranks. "This is what comes of allowing immature girls inside a hospital. This sort of foolishness. Mrs. Brent and Mrs. Collins shall most certainly have a full report from me. At once!"

She bent down stiffly and yanked at one of the bed handles. There was a faint crack and the handle began to turn, gradually settling the bed into proper position. The other handle also responded to her authoritative pressure. The bed was normally level now.

"Come with me, young lady!" Miss Winters ordered, beckoning to Bonnie with a thin finger.

"Me!" Bonnie squeaked. "But I——"

"I saw what you did," Miss Winters said.

"But—but—" Bonnie faced the others desperately. Surely they would not let her take the blame.

Denise gulped. "M-Miss Winters," she croaked. "I—it was I——"

"Me, too," Pixie said, valiantly taking a step forward. "Bonnie had nothing to do with it.

She—we got the bed up and couldn't get it to go down, and Bonnie tried to help."

"Indeed? She would have done the hospital greater service by reporting you two at once, instead of remaining a party to your foolishness."

"It didn't start as foolishness," Denise declared bravely, tears glistening in her eyes. "I —well, I'm kind of dense sometimes about getting the hang of things. And I've had trouble remembering about the bed cranks. I mean, the right one for the head and the left one—oh, dear! I mean, it's the other way around! See what I mean? And we thought—*I* thought—— Well, here was this empty bed, and it seemed a good time to practice. Honestly, that's how it happened, before we—I mean, I, turned silly."

Her eyes were beseeching, and Bonnie thought that the stern-faced supervisor's mouth twitched slightly. Miss Winters seemed silent for a long time, studying each uncomfortable young face in turn. "Very well," she said at last. "I shall overlook this But I warn you, nonsense will not be tolerated here, and I shall remember you girls. Get on with your work." She spun about and marched out on silent, rubber-soled feet, leaving the door wide open.

"Oh-h, glory. I thought I'd die!" Denise said. "She petrifies me."

"Mean old witch," Mavis said, reaching for a folded sheet and giving it a vicious shake.

Bonnie, too, seethed with resentment. Who did Miss Winters think she was, anyway! Here they were volunteers—donating their time— and she treated them in this high and mighty manner. She might at least have shown some understanding, after things were explained to her.

The girls finished their bedmaking in a sober mood and reported back an hour later.

"My, but you're a solemn lot," Miss Kent said as they stood in front of the Nurse's Station.

"Yes, aren't they?" Miss Winters' harsh voice grazed past them meaningfully.

"I felt her icy breath," Pixie said afterward. "And heard her teeth gnash. I hope I never have to work on that floor again!"

Mrs. Brent assigned the other girls elsewhere, but to her dismay Bonnie was asked to remain on Fourth, under Miss Winters' suspicious eyes. It seemed to her that every time the supervisor looked at her, it was with disapproval. Bonnie had the uncomfortable feeling that they would never get along.

She did not have too much time to brood about it, though, for she was kept busy running errands and answering patients' signals. The incredibly old lady in 424 wanted another pitcher of ice water. She seemed fretful and kept picking at her coverlet with bony fingers. Bonnie thought she'd better check on the request and brought the water after Miss Kent okayed it.

"I'm ninety-eight!" the patient quavered as Bonnie poured her a glassful, "and I'm not going to go till I'm a hundred. That fool doctor might as well get it through his head. . . ."

"Yes, ma'am," Bonnie said and escaped, as the old lady lapsed into unintelligible mutterings.

The man in 405 wanted her to buy him some cigarettes, but he didn't look at all well and there was some strange equipment beside his bed. When Bonnie relayed his request to Miss Kent, the nurse looked horrified and set off down the hall to lay the law down to him.

When she returned, she said, "He's been in and out of an oxygen mask all day. If he ever lit a cigarette with the oxygen on we'd have a flash fire on the floor, and goodness knows what would happen to him. I thought I had explained it to him before. There's a sign on his door forbidding smoking in that room. Didn't you see it?"

Bonnie's face reddened as she shook her head. From now on she would be on the lookout for such things and she thanked her stars the incident had not occurred while Miss Winters was around.

The light over 416 went on and Bonnie hurried away to see what was wanted there. The lady in the bed near the window had dropped her book, and her companion wanted her bed lowered so she could take a nap. Bonnie pulled out the crank and rotated it carefully, and as she turned away she saw Miss Winters in the doorway watching her. It flustered Bonnie so that she forgot to push in the bed crank again. Miss Winters' sharp chin came up and she brushed past her and clanked the handle in pointedly, making Bonnie wish she could fall right through to the next floor. On the other hand, it would have been pleasant to have the floor open up under Miss Winters!

"Bonnie!" It was Miss Kent calling and Bonnie hurried away gratefully. "This cart of supplies is to be returned to CSR. And here's a requisition for fresh sterile supplies. Do you know where to go?"

"Yes. Third floor."

Miss Kent smiled at her and Bonnie forgot Miss Winters for the moment as she rolled the cart toward the padded service elevators.

She had no trouble finding the Central Supply Room where she returned the used equipment at one window and moved to the next with her requisition. Among other things she received two glass flasks, which she put carefully on the bottom shelf of the cart, as she had been taught, and then she was ready to return.

Just as the elevator came, a patient was wheeled toward the Delivery Room. Overcome by curiosity, Bonnie turned her head, at the same time pushing the cart into the waiting elevator. But she had forgotten to press the "hold" button, and the door began to close. She saw it out of the corner of her eye and panicked. Should she push the cart faster or yank it back? In that moment of indecision the cart was stuck and the glass flasks clanked together and rocked perilously.

Bonnie was ready to cry. What more could happen to her today! She was tempted to leave the cart right there and run home—all the way. Frantically she glanced over her shoulder toward the Nurse's Station, but there was no one behind the desk to help her at the moment. And then a big, comfortable colored woman in a white uniform was at her side, giving the elevator door a firm push backward and a yank to the stuck cart.

As she turned gratefully, Bonnie recognized Vernella Potter, the practical nurse everyone affectionately called Nellie Belle. Nancy had pointed her out in the halls and told Bonnie about Nellie Belle's big heart and sunny disposition. Nellie Belle's white teeth flashed in a smile as she leaned in and pushed the "hold" button on the elevator.

"Those pesky doors," she said. "If you don't watch out, they'll nip your nose right off—and on me they're liable to nip off a whole lot more, too, front and back!" She slapped her enormous hips and laughed. "Where to, honey?"

"Fourth," Bonnie said, breathing a sigh of relief. "And thank you so much."

Nellie Belle's eyes twinkled. She released the "hold" button and pressed the floor for Bonnie and then waved as the doors closed. What a darling she was. Nancy had said that whenever anybody needed mothering, Nellie Belle was assigned to the case. No wonder.

The rest of Bonnie's first day on her own passed without further incident. Miss Kent was kind and considerate, and if it hadn't been for Miss Winters, Bonnie would have found her duties pleasant. Every time she saw the supervisor go by it cast a spell over whatever she was doing. At five o'clock she marked down her first eight hours of duty and felt as though she had been baptized in fire.

It had been a long day, and as she found a seat on the bus she realized how much of it she had spent on her feet. Perhaps Mother had been right. Perhaps this was going to be too much for her.

But when she recounted the adventures of "her day" to Laura, she began to see everything in a different light. Even the incident of the "broken bed" became funny in retrospect. And as for getting stuck in the elevator—"I'd give anything to meet Nellie Belle!" Laura exclaimed enviously. "She sounds absolutely marvelous. Oh, you lucky, lucky thing, Bonnie!"

The account, as she repeated it later at the dinner table for her parents' benefit, however, omitted the first incident, and touched briefly on the second.

"Well, you do seem to be enjoying this work," Mother said. "But if it gets to be too much for you——" She stopped at the look Father sent her.

Quite obviously her father did not expect Bonnie to be a quitter, and her cheeks flamed as she recalled the awful moment when she wanted to leave the stuck cart and run home to mother! She had not mentioned that even to Laura. And what would Dad have thought of it! Thank goodness Nellie Belle had come along when she did.

seven

THE NEXT FEW DAYS WERE CONSIDERABLY LESS hectic and Bonnie began to feel more at home in the Center. A great many interesting things were going on in the hospital, and there were so many different people with whom she came in contact. There were the paid assistants, college girls for the most part, working for tuition money. One of them was Jan Peterson, from Highlands, Colorado, who was taking a four-year degree course in nursing. She had been a junior nurse's aide in a small thirty-bed hospital, where the girls were given a great deal more training than was allowed junior volunteers elsewhere.

Highlands Hospital was so shorthanded, that the girls actually gave some bedside care. They were taught how to take temperatures and respiration readings, to assist with occupational therapy, help plan hospital menus, and after checking out on twenty-seven hospital procedures, the final requirement was to observe a surgical operation and the delivery of a baby!

"Our reward was a perky little cap and an awfully good feeling," Jan told Bonnie one day as they inspected surgical gowns in Central Supply, sorting them for repair or sterilization from a huge clean laundry cart.

"I'd be scared to death!" Bonnie said.

"By the operation or the baby?" Jan shook her head. "Not if you were one of us. Most of the girls came from farm families where they had already seen animals born, and where they often had to assist with the birthing or care of sick animals. Watching a human baby born was the greatest thrill I ever had. It seemed a culmination of everything I had learned. That and watching the competence and calmness of the OR staff during the operation. I decided then and there that I wanted to be a nurse, too.

"I think I'll go back home, to Highlands, where they can really use me. It's a windswept little town that serves a huge rural area. It's fiendishly hot in summer, and deadly cold in winter, and the wind never seems to stop blowing. But I was born there and I love it. The wind is music to my ears, so I won't mind it. Nurses who come from—well, gentler climes, shall we say?" She laughed. "They never last. I will."

Bonnie listened to Jan in wonder. Was it Mrs. Brent or Mrs. Collins who had said this junior nurse's aides program was national? Somehow, until now she had not realized that it was so widespread.

Bonnie had told Pixie about her encounter with Nellie Belle, and during lunch that day Pixie mentioned that she'd heard they had a very sick little boy in Hartwell. "Your friend has been with him practically night and day, holding him in this world. A couple of nurses were talking about it," Pixie sounded awed. "That woman is a sort of legend around here."

Bonnie was curious to see Nellie Belle in action, so after lunch she slipped out to one of the visitors' ramps lining the contagion wing. She had no idea where Nellie Belle might be, but as she walked along the line of carefully screened windows, she heard a crooning sound and paused.

There was Nellie Belle, sitting in a chair with a limp little boy in her lap, rocking him and singing softly to him. She had been doing it for hours and looked as if she would continue for hours more if this was the comfort the child needed. Bonnie felt the sting of tears in her eyes, and as she turned away she said a prayer for the small patient. "Please, please, God. Let him get well."

The next morning, when she came in, she rather fearfully inquired about the little boy.

"Oh, Jimmie's going to be all right," the Pink Lady at the Information Desk told her. "Our Nellie Belle just loved him well," she added, smiling. "He passed the crisis right in her arms, and the doctor says he will mend fast."

"Thank you!" Bonnie's heart was suddenly light. The small and unknown Jimmie might have been her own little brother. When she left the desk she was sure that Nellie Belle's Tender Loving Care—a standard prescription, especially in Pediatrics—was as much responsible for Jimmie's recovery as the medicines the doctor gave him.

As she walked past the revolving door of the lobby, a distracted couple burst through and Bonnie stopped, startled.

"Where—where's Joanie?" the woman asked

incoherently, and the man put an arm around her to quiet her.

"Our daughter," he said, trying to keep from showing the emotional stress he was under. "Joanie Simmons. Sh-she was hit by a truck. Th-they—the hospital called us."

Bonnie listened, horrified. This was the first time she had ever been brought so close to tragedy. What should she tell them? Her uniform made them think she knew something. Bonnie looked around wildly, and evidently understanding her panic the pink-smocked adult volunteer at the desk hurried over and took charge. Bonnie stumbled away toward Mrs. Brent's office.

"What's wrong?" Mrs. Brent asked, rising as Bonnie appeared in the doorway. "Are you ill?"

Bonnie shook her head. She sat down abruptly and then explained about Joanie's parents.

"Oh, yes," the Director of Volunteers said. "Joanie was riding her bicycle when she was struck down. They brought her in a short while ago. She's up in surgery now."

Mrs. Brent laid a gentle hand on Bonnie's shoulder. "This is a hospital, dear. Here we face joy and sorrow a dozen times every day. Someone gets well—and someone else does not. A child is born—a child dies. Whatever the outcome, we can at least find comfort in know-

ing that we—all of us—did our best for every
individual in our care."

"Yes," Bonnie murmured, trying to take
heart. Lucky Jimmie. Poor Joanie.

Bonnie drew Second Floor duty the next
day, and saw Joanie lying in a big white bed in
the Quiet Room for the critically ill. The little
girl's parents sat motionless beside her, their
hands clasped, their faces drawn.

Two days later she met them in the lobby,
looking quite cheerful. So Joanie must be on
the mend, Bonnie thought. Mr. Simmons noticed her, smiled and nodded. Impulsively Bonnie went over to them. "I'm so glad Joanie is
better," she said.

Mrs. Simmons looked up. "Thank you, dear."
Her face was gentle and sweet. Her husband
nodded warmly. Both of them seemed to have
cast a great weight from their shoulders.

But that afternoon, when Bonnie slipped
down to Second to take a peek at Joanie, her
bed was empty and made up fresh to receive
a new patient. With a clutch at her heart Bonnie stopped a passing nurse and asked, "Where's
Joanie?"

The nurse looked startled, then shook her
head. "She didn't make it . . . internal injuries
. . . a sudden change. . . ."

Bonnie wished she had never heard of Joanie

Simmons, never met her parents, never come to the Medical Center in the first place. Was nursing always like this? Did nurses feel so deeply for every patient? She certainly would not want any part of that! She slipped into the nurses' lavatory and dabbed water on her eyes. Why did anyone ever want to be a nurse!

The afternoon was very quiet, for which she was grateful. There were no errands to run and after she had helped pass out fresh ice water, there seemed nothing to do. Bonnie felt so low that she decided to sign out early, and when she left she was not sure that she would ever come back again.

Outside, on the hospital grounds, Pixie caught up with her. "Hi, Bon! What're you doing tonight?"

"Nothing, as usual," Bonnie said dispiritedly. "With Rock away at summer camp I couldn't be more dateless."

"Me, too." Pixie sighed. "My Tommy managed to flunk Latin and Chemistry so thoroughly that his family packed him off to summer school in New Hampshire, where the fellows are tutored to within a thousandth of an inch of their brain capacity. How about you and me having a wild fling tonight? Let's go to the movies. There's a musical at the Community, and I'm just in the mood for some plush living surrounded by dozens of handsome young men, the way those movie stars in musicals always are. How about it?"

Bonnie hesitated. Still, she had nothing better to do—and it would be good to get the hospital out of her system.

"Well? Is the great mind made up?" Pixie asked.

"Oh! Yes. Where'll I meet you?"

"How about Abbott's for a soda first? We might pick up some other kids there and make it a party for the first show."

"Fine! And here comes my bus! I'll see you there at six-fifteen." As she climbed aboard, Bonnie wished she had made plans to have dinner with Pixie. The way she felt at the moment, she didn't want to talk to the family; certainly not to Mother, who would know instantly that the hospital had been awful today and might even insist that she resign.

Resign! Bonnie sat up a little straighter. Well, why not? And yet the thought made her uncomfortable. After the eagerness with which she had talked her family into letting her sign up? Mother would not be sorry, of course. But Dad . . . and Laura! Bonnie could see her sister's unhappy face if she told her she was resigning from the Candy Stripers.

Dad would think she was a quitter—quietly,

but none the less emphatically. He always said they should never start anything they did not plan to finish. Well, of course, she wasn't interested in nursing, especially after today! Still, she'd have to stick it out. Before she got off the bus, Bonnie very carefully put on a cheerful face to wear home, and when she told about her day at the hospital, she skimmed over the details. It had been a slow day—that was why she was home early—and no one questioned her.

She changed to a favorite blue dress, and by the time she reached Abbott's she was feeling a bit better. Denise was there with several girls from school who were not Candy Stripers, and so they were told all about the hospital experiences. In the midst of an excited recital by Pixie, Denise chanted, "What you see there, What you hear there, Let it stay there, When you leave there."

"What's that?" Edith Hurd asked. "A secret password?"

"In a way." Pixie's eyes were dancing. "Denise was just telling me I was talking too much. We have our ethics to observe," she added primly.

"Our lips are sealed," Bonnie added, falling into the spirit of the thing, suddenly feeling very close to Pixie and Denise.

"From here to here—with adhesive tape,"

Pixie amplified, pantomiming, "if we're caught spilling hospital secrets to outsiders!"

"Well, gee whiz!" Edith and Alice Prout exclaimed together—and then it was time to get their tickets for the first show.

It was fun to be out with the girls after so much of nothing but hospital atmosphere, and Bonnie agreed eagerly when Pixie said, "We must do this more often. Us summer widows must stick together!"

eight

FROM TIME TO TIME EVERY CANDY STRIPER HAD to serve on Courier Duty. "That is to keep you girls in touch with other parts of the hospital," Mrs. Brent explained. "Some of you establish yourselves in one or two areas and tend to lose sight of the others. The hospital is composed of many vital departments working together to help people get well. On Courier you get to see every department.

"Bonnie Schuyler, Pixie Chase, Mavis Watts, and Paula Palmer, suppose you take Courier for Wednesday. All right?"

"Wednesday!" Bonnie said, making a quick

calculation in her head. "I'll have my first hundred-hour star."

"Goody for you!" Pixie exclaimed. "Then everybody can see it."

"Absolutely!" Mrs. Brent smiled. "Everybody!"

The Couriers assembled in the Women Volunteers room on the fifth floor and waited for the telephone calls which would send them scurrying on a variety of errands. Proudly wearing her first one-hundred-hour star, Bonnie acted as captain at the desk. As the call came in she jotted down the department calling, the time, the name of the person dispatched, and then the time of her return. On a busy day the calls got way ahead of the girls, but on this Wednesday they were only moderately busy. Pixie sat in an easy chair, doing a crossword puzzle in a magazine. Mavis and Paula Palmer, who was the newest recruit and wore too much make-up, were in a huddle on the couch, talking and giggling.

"What's another word for lacquer?" Pixie asked. "This puzzle's hard."

Paula glanced at her. "You mean, like nail polish?" She extended her own manicured hands, the extra long nails covered with gleaming scarlet.

"Wow!" Pixie stared. "You look as if you've

been dabbling in surgery without your gloves on, Paula!"

The other girl shuddered. "That's a place you'll never get me near, unless I'm carried there unconscious."

"But how do you get away with polish like that? Hasn't Mrs. Brent said anything to you about it?" Bonnie asked.

"Oh, sure. She and Mrs. Collins. But I don't care. They're getting my services for free, aren't they? So if I want to wear bright red polish, I will."

The shocked silence told Paula she had said too much, and too crudely. Her face turned as red as her nails. "A-ah," she said, shrugging, "this Candy Striping wasn't my idea. It's my mother's. She thinks I ought to be a nurse, and I don't. I want to be a beautician. But no, she always wanted to be a nurse and didn't get there, so I have to be."

"Cheer up," Pixie said. "Feeling the way you do, you'll never make it."

"Suits me. That's what I want to prove to her. I hope they fire me from here, and then maybe she'll be convinced."

Mavis moved restlessly. "This is boring. I hate Courier when there's nothing doing—not even any cute interns or doctors going to the meeting room past our door. Did you kids know that all the rooms on both sides of this hall belong to the interns? We sure have some cuties. Have any of you met—oh-h-hh!" She stopped, staring through the open door, and then got up and ran and peered around it.

"Did you see him?" she breathed. "That was Dr. Ricci!" She rolled her eyes. "Is he ever handsome. A real dreamboat."

"My goodness, do you always run after him and stare?" Pixie asked.

"Every chance I get," Mavis admitted baldly. "And Dr. Celestin, the French one they call Dr. Tin-tin. He's little, but boy is he charming. I think he's on ambulance duty."

"I go for him too," was Paula's retort. "Only if I needed an ambulance doctor, I'd get stuck with Guthrie."

"Dr. Guthrie!" Bonnie exclaimed. "He scares me, too. But he's the Resident, and I don't think they ever go out on ambulance cases." To her Dr. Tom Guthrie was a bit like Miss Winters. She was sure he, too, disapproved of Candy Stripers. It seemed to her that he always glowered when she went past him.

"Dr. Tom is so homely, he's fascinating," Mavis said, stretching lazily. "That craggy face of his is too serious, though. He never looks to the right or left." She wrinkled her nose.

"Oh, no? He looks up on Fourth when that

Rocheen Kent walks by. Not a frank and open stare but as if he couldn't help watching her and didn't want her to know he couldn't," Paula said.

Mavis sat forward, scenting romance. "Go on!"

"Well, the beautiful Rocheen knows, just the same. I've seen her turn pink and flustered."

"Ah! Romance among the medics," Pixie said callously. "I still want a word for lacquer."

She never got it, because at that moment the telephone rang, and from then on it did not seem to be still for more than two minutes at a time. Couriers were in demand on every floor. Special diets had to be taken to the kitchen on the ground floor. Pediatrics needed supplies from CSR. Flowers, in what seemed like carloads, were arriving for Maternity. Three patients at once needed to go down to Physio for treatments, and there were two waiting for X-ray.

The orders got way ahead of Bonnie and she kept the girls running. Just as Pixie returned, quite winded after a bout with a youngster for X-ray who screamed all the way there and back, the phone rang again.

The call was for a courier to take a patient's specimen from Fourth to the general lab on First. *"Stat!"* the nurse said into the telephone. In hospital parlance it meant, "Right away. Urgent. Come on the double. Rush!" The specimen would have to be tested immediately.

Bonnie jotted down the time of the call, wrote in her own name, put Pixie in charge of the phone and hurried away, without running.

Miss Kent handed Bonnie the test tube with a wad of cotton stuck in the top like a solid plume of white smoke, and gave her the slip for the laboratory report.

"Take this in directly and tell them *stat*," she repeated, her face serious. "And be *very* careful." She looked, Bonnie thought, almost as if she wished to take the specimen down herself.

"I'll be careful," she promised.

"All right."

Bonnie turned and found Miss Emma Winters standing behind her. Bonnie's lips moved in a mechanical smile as she moved off toward the elevators.

She pressed the "pass" button, and arrived, express, in the lobby on the first floor. A fresh load of flowers was being delivered, and some of the bouquets were so beautiful, she glanced back for another look. The next instant her feet seemed to be flying out from under her! She fell sidewise, and instinctively supported herself on one elbow.

"*Oh!*" Frantically Bonnie clutched the test

tube; she must not let it fall, and as suddenly she was caught in a pair of strong arms and reset firmly on her feet.

Her first thought was for the test tube. Seeing that all was well, she turned to her rescuer.

A tall young man, dressed in a white lab coat looked down at her out of amused gray eyes in a clean-cut face. "Almost took a spill, didn't you, Star Girl," he said, flicking a finger at the new blue star pinned to her pinafore bib.

"Yes," Bonnie said, her heart still hammering from the near disaster. "Thanks. 'Scuse me, but I have to deliver this in a hurry."

She whisked into the lab and sniffed at its indefinable odors as she put the test tube into a technician's steady hands.

"Isn't this your requisition slip?" the girl asked as Bonnie was about to leave.

She glanced at the yellow slip the girl held out. She hadn't realized that Miss Kent had given her a slip for a return errand. "Shall I wait?" she asked.

"No. Go into the next room and David Adams will give you what you need." She called out instructions and a male voice replied, "Okay. Will do."

Again Bonnie found herself facing the young man she had met so precipitously in the hall.

"Hi," he said. "How do you feel, Star Girl? Still shaken?"

"No. That tube's safe, so I'm all right. I don't know what they would have done to me if I'd smashed it."

His smile stopped midway and he reached out to pull her arm away from her side. "You've skinned your elbow. It's bleeding. Better buzz down to the clinic and have it patched up."

Bonnie inspected the damage. "It's nothing. Really." She dabbed at it with a tissue.

"Tsk, tsk," he chided. "Most unsanitary. If you look at the slides under those microscopes," he pointed to the row on a table behind him, "you won't treat skin breaks so casually. Have you any idea how fast bacteria multiplies? To the clinic, young lady. Can I trust you to go by yourself, or shall I escort you?"

Bonnie bristled. She wasn't going to be "escorted" like a real accident case. "I'll go," she said. "Thanks anyway."

"That's better. I'll put these tubes you want in a paper bag so you can take them along and deliver them later. " He picked off the glass vials from a pegged rack near a deep metal sink.

Bonnie hurried down the stairs, one flight, and angled toward OPD, the Out Patient Department. Just where was she supposed to go?

She had never revisited this area since her tour. She must have looked vague, for a nurse, walking by asked her what she wanted and then directed her toward a small office.

"Bonnie!" Nancy rose from behind a desk where she had been writing. "What are you doing down here?"

"Playing patient," Bonnie said, holding up her arm. "I fell and did this."

"M'mmm. Looks like a nasty scrape."

It was, Bonnie realized with some surprise. The bruise was beginning to sting. Nancy slipped out of the room and a moment later was back, followed by a short, slight man who managed to look dapper even in his white intern's coat and trousers. He had a wisp of a mustache, and although he was far from handsome, his smile added a delightful warmth to his face.

"Ah!" he said, and the exclamation was heavily accented. "What have we here? An injured Candee Striper. One of your friends, Nancee?"

"Yes, Dr. Celestin. My next-door neighbor. She's skinned her arm."

So this was the French intern, nicknamed Dr. Tin-tin, that she'd heard about.

He lifted her elbow gently. "How did it happen?" he asked, as if hers were a major injury. She said something to that effect, and he pursed his lips and answered, "To the one who has the hurt, no matter how trivial, it is serious. *Major*." And then he laughed, as if they shared a joke between them. "Come," he said, taking her into a treatment room. He rubbed the bruised area hard with his fingers and Bonnie winced. "Now we know there are no bone splinters. How did this happen?" he asked again.

Feeling rather foolish, Bonnie told him, and as she talked, Nancy wrote the information down on a large white card.

"For goodness sakes," Bonnie said, "I wouldn't have even come down here if that David Adams up in the lab had not been so insistent."

"Quite rightly, too," Nancy said, sounding very professional. She held up the white card. "Now you have a clinic chart—in case you ever have to come here for treatment again."

Dr. Celestin touched the wound with disinfectant and put a band-aid over it.

Bonnie eyed it with amusement. "After all that don't I get a splint and an arm sling?"

"Neurotic, isn't she?" Nancy and Dr. Tin-tin laughed companionably. "That's all, Miss," he said. "Away with you—or would you like to see the Clinic? We're awfully proud of it."

"I would," Bonnie said, "but I do have to get back. Maybe just a quick look-see? Thank you, Doctor."

"Not at all." Dr. Celestin bowed. He sounded a little like Charles Boyer.

As Nancy showed her the treatment rooms, the well-equipped accident receiving room, the "minor" emergency operating room, and the "fracture room"—"where we set broken bones," Bonnie became so fascinated she forgot she was supposed to return to the fourth floor and to her Courier duties as well!

The tour was interrupted when a nurse spotted them down the hall and called out, "Is there a Courier down here?"

Bonnie started guiltily. "Yes!" she called back in a small voice.

"Well, they're wondering on Fourth what has become of you!" The nurse's voice sounded tart.

"Oh, glory!" Bonnie clutched her bag of tubes. "I'll bet it's Miss Winters who's doing the wondering. G'by, Nancy. Thanks for the tour!"

On the fourth floor Miss Emma Winters looked as if she had been pacing in front of the elevators, switching her broomstick. She almost snatched the bag of tubes from Bonnie and then rasped, "What happened to you?"

Her face scarlet, Bonnie said, "I—I fell," and pointed to the band-aid on her arm.

Miss Winters frowned. "Does it take that long to put on a band-aid? Were you running? Well, never mind. These—*girls!*"

She says it as if it's a crime to be young, Bonnie thought resentfully. There was no justice or understanding in that woman. No human quality. Bonnie stomped angrily up the stairs to the Volunteers room.

But things had slowed down there. Paula was sitting at the desk and Carol was with her. "Hello," Paula said. "We thought you'd got lost. Want to go to lunch? Carol just came in to see if she could relieve any of us. Maternity is very inactive today. Mavis and Pixie went down to the cafeteria, so you can go, too, if you want."

"All right," Bonnie nodded. She was glad to get away, for she was in no mood to talk to Paula or Carol and have to give any explanations.

Pixie and Mavis were sitting near the dining room door and waved at her as she came in. They already had their food, so she and Ginny Lou, who was just behind her, got trays and moved toward the tempting array of eatables. Ginny Lou gazed mournfully at the desserts as she confined herself to a salad, a cheese sandwich and a glass of milk.

"I've started my diet," she said, sounding weak with hunger. "Mrs. Brent and Mrs. Collins really went to work on me, explaining how awful it is to be overweight. They even showed me what fat looks like. Ugh!" She shuddered. "But the real argument," she confessed as they made their way down the rows of tables, "was that I couldn't stand up to nurse's training, carting all this weight around. My feet couldn't take it, Mrs. Collins said." Ginny sounded as if she thought that would be worse than death. "So, after I promised to stick to a diet, they had Dr. Guthrie check me over and prescribe for me—and he's going to weigh me every single week—himself! And I couldn't bear to have him glower at me if I backslide. He expects me to lose a pound and a half a week, so I'd better, even if it kills me. I got the impression he will carve it off of me himself, if I don't. I'm beginning to think he scares patients into getting well or into doing what he wants."

Her recital had elements of humor, but this was serious business to her, so Bonnie resisted the impulse to laugh. She even gave up cake for dessert, for Ginny's sake.

They had just seated themselves with Mavis and Pixie when David Adams came into the dining room. Bonnie saw him at once—saw how good looking and clean-cut he was, how clear his gray eyes, and with what determination he slicked down the faint wave in his fair hair. She realized she was staring, and looked down quickly, but not fast enough to escape his attention.

He smiled and came straight to her. "How are you? How's the arm?" Thank goodness he had not called her "Star Girl" or she'd be saddled with that nickname forever, Bonnie thought, her face turning pink.

"Fine," she said hastily. "They fixed it up in the Clinic."

"Good!" He glanced at the other girls, and Bonnie decided that introductions were in order, especially the way Mavis was beaming the thought at her. She ran through the names. Now he knew the others' but not hers! His eyes crinkled quizzically, as if he were thinking the same thing. But he said nothing.

"Join us!" Mavis invited boldly, patting an empty chair.

"Thanks," David said, "but the fellows are waiting for me over there." He tipped his head and the girls looked toward the long table near the windows where a group of boys were seated. "See you later."

"We-ell, Still Waters Schuyler," Mavis began

at once, "where did you glaum onto him? And
what's this about your arm, darling? Such concern over a teeny-weeny band-aid! Come on,
give!"

Why did she have to blush, Bonnie thought
furiously. Mavis would not be put off, once she
started worming something out. "I don't know
a thing about him, beyond his name," she said
firmly, "and the fact that he was in the lab
when I slipped and almost smashed a specimen I
was carrying. He—saw me. That's all."

"Ye-es?" Mavis' brows arched. "I bet he
caught you. Ha! I knew I was right. What are
you getting so pink for?"

"Oh, Mavis, hush," Ginny Lou said. "You're
embarrassing Bonnie."

Mavis rolled her eyes toward the long table
near the window. "Must be part of the college crowd here for the summer. Young medics
so eager to get started, they're willing to scrub
the OR on their hands and knees, and be orderlies and porters! Since you saw him in the lab,
maybe he's going to be a technician. I wish we
could really get to know those boys. Real college
men!"

"Down, Mavis, down," Pixie said. "You are a
riot. No maidenly reserve at all."

"Huh. What did that ever get you?" Mavis
retorted, getting to her feet and displaying her

figure to its best advantage. The boys at the long table however were completely absorbed in some discussion of their own. Mavis shrugged as she sauntered out of the cafeteria.

The afternoon was fairly busy for the Couriers. There were more patients to be taken down to X-ray; to "physio," the Physical Therapy department, for electrical therapy treatments, whirlpool baths, and exercises such as walking up and down a short flight of stairs, or between parallel bars used for support.

Mavis begged for the trips to the lab, and returned from one errand quite disgruntled. "That David Adams is a snob," she muttered. "You can have him." She tossed her dark hair back and sat down with a thump.

"We didn't know he was yours to give," Pixie said. "What did he do to you?"

"Nothing," Mavis grumbled. "He acted as if he'd never seen me before. You'd better play hard to get, Bonnie. I think he's that kind."

"I have no intention of playing anything for his benefit," Bonnie replied coldly. "And I'll thank you to mind your own business."

At the end of the day she was tired and hot. July in Hamilton was quite different from July at the shore. She thought about their beach house longingly and sighed. She had been on her feet a great deal today, and her head ached, too. Although she had been on the job several weeks now, she still worried about making mistakes, especially around Miss Winters. This was one night she'd be glad to get home.

As she walked out into the corridor near the elevator, a nurse gave her some last minute errands to do. Bonnie hurried through them, but even so she missed the Longview Avenue bus. It's taillights were disappearing when she stepped out of the lobby entrance. A half hour she had to wait! And she felt as if she couldn't stand another minute. She sat down on the concrete parapet, quite wilted.

Cars glided past her in the circular drive. She wished they would move faster; that might make a breeze.

"Hello, Star Girl!"

nine

SHE LOOKED UP TO SEE DAVID ADAMS CLIMBING OUT
of an ancient convertible. A purely feminine
thought darted through her mind: *How do I
look?*

"Tired?" he asked sympathetically. "Are you
waiting for someone to pick you up?"

She shook her head and mentioned the missed
bus.

"Don't give it another thought. My chariot is
at your service."

But she held back. He was not a stranger
exactly, and yet she didn't really know him or
anything about him.

He stood there, with his head cocked, looking down at her. "Would you feel better if I dragged Dr. Page, president of the medical staff, out here to introduce us formally? Or the hospital director?"

She felt silly then, and let him take her arm and guide her to his decrepit little car.

"Be thankful it's not raining," he remarked, getting in on the other side. "This is only a half-convertible. The top does not go up."

She laughed, and he asked, "Where to, Star Girl—or am I never to know your name?"

"By all means know my name," she said. "It's Bonnie Schuyler."

"Pretty. Suits you. And I like your nice hair."

Her pony tail had come down in the afternoon and she had not taken the trouble to put it up again. It hung in the simplest of hair-do's. Apparently David liked it that way, and she was pleased and flattered by this older boy's attention. He must be at least—well, twenty. Maybe even older. Twenty-two? And awfully *nice*. Mavis was crazy.

"You live—where?" David prompted.

She gave him the directions. "What about you? I hope I'm not taking you too far out of your way."

He grimaced. "I'm at the YMCA in town. It's not precisely home, but it'll do."

"Where is home?"

"Chicago. Too far to commute."

"I should say. What are you doing way out here at Hamilton?" Bonnie asked shyly.

"Getting experience. Like the other fellows. You see, Bonnie, I hope to be a hospital administrator someday. That means four years of college, and then two years of graduate work in hospital administration, plus all kinds of hospital experience beyond that. It's an awfully important post, as you can probably imagine. So, I want to hurry up the experience by getting as much of it as I can summers. I plan to work in different hospitals throughout the country and see how they operate. Here I help in the lab, washing tubes and flasks and slides mostly, and sometimes make the simplest of tests. I've gone in pretty heavily for chemistry and biology in school, so I'm useful to them in a limited sort of way. Sometimes I go down to physical therapy and assist there, or wherever I'm useful. It's fascinating work, Bonnie. I feel as if I'm working with—well, life itself. To me a hospital is a big Laboratory for Living."

She was spellbound and a little breathless, and suddenly glad that she was wearing a Candy Striper's uniform. David talked so differently from anyone she had ever known. Why, Rock Caldwell wouldn't even understand what he was talking about!

"Did I bore you?" David asked, sounding rueful.

"No, no! Not at all. I think your plans are wonderful—David?" She sampled the name tentatively.

"Of course, 'David,'" he said, smiling. "I don't stand on ceremony with Star Girls whom I catch in mid-air and bully into going to the clinic."

They laughed—and there was her house, coming up much too fast. She toyed with the idea of asking him in to meet her family— but then it seemed too soon. Such short acquaintance. Perhaps she had better tell her family about him first.

"Right here," she said, indicating the Schuyler drive. "Thank you very much—David." The name was strange and sweet on her tongue.

"That's all right, Bonnie. It was a pleasure." He waved, spun the wheel, and the little car chugged away.

Bonnie watched it disappear dreamily. David was—oh, so *nice*. And he treated her as if she were quite grown-up. His own age, in fact—because she was a Candy Striper. She patted her uniform.

Suddenly she became aware of someone watching her from next door. Cliff Coburn! He seemed faintly amused. What had her face revealed? She tilted her chin. "Hello, Clifford," she said regally, and swept up the walk. He was such a child in comparison to David. To think that she had been even slightly interested in *him!*

Laura met her at the door. "Who was that fellow who brought you home? A doctor? An intern?" she demanded.

"Of course not." Bonnie shook her off. "Just a boy who works at the hospital. I'll tell you about him later. Let me cool off first." She ran up the stairs. Strange how cool she had felt in David's car, and not tired at all.

She came down to dinner, her hair brushed down the way David liked it.

"Who was he?" Laura mouthed the words from her place across the table.

"Who was who?" Mother asked.

"The absolutely scrumptious fellow who brought Bonnie home. Wait till Rock Caldwell hears about him!"

"Laura! That will do," Mother said severely. "Rock has no right to set any limits whatsoever on Bonnie's friends. I'm glad he's away this summer. That boy's been underfoot here much too much. Who did bring you home?"

Bonnie glared at Laura. Why did her sister always have to precipitate things! She told her family about David, leaving out her own odd feeling toward him.

"Sounds like a solid citizen, all right," her father commented. "Bring him around sometime."

"Yes, do," Mother said.

"Is David going to be your boy friend?" Laura broke in before her sister could answer.

"Don't be silly!" Bonnie had not meant to snap but it came out that way. "He's just somebody I know at the hospital. Don't go getting any ideas."

"What's silly about it? I only asked."

"That will do, Laura." Father patted his younger daughter's hand with an air of finality.

"Well, if you ask me, I think he——"

"*Laura!*" Bonnie's voice was a muffled shriek. Her sister's eyes went wide, but she subsided.

Their parents exchanged a silent, puzzled look.

Now there was a real reason for hurrying to the Medical Center: David. Since they both worked in different areas, Bonnie never knew when she might run into him. When they did meet, he did not always stop to talk, but he always smiled with a special warmth, she thought.

There was that wonderful day she and David were assigned to "Physio." Wearing the white duck uniform of the orderly, he lifted patients to treatment tables and into the seat in front of the whirlpool tank. Bonnie busied herself covering the tables with fresh linen after each patient had left, even laying out some of the equipment for treatments under the kindly direction of "Uncle George," the head of the department.

She listened respectfully, during a lull, as he told them of the remarkable accomplishments of physical therapy—how people, who seemed hopelessly crippled, learned to walk again, or to use their hands, how flaccid muscles were given exercise until they were able to do their job unaided. David seemed to understand the technical terms "Uncle George" used, and Bonnie, standing beside him, tried to look intelligent.

Nellie Belle brought a tiny, long-term patient down from Pediatrics and jollied him into a series of exercises with hand pulleys, something no one else had been able to accomplish without rivers of tears from the thin, big-eyed tyke.

"She's the biggest asset Pediatrics ever had," one of the therapists whispered. "I don't know what the hospital would do without her."

"Think you'd like to be a physical therapist, Bonnie?" David asked as they were on their way to lunch.

She had never given it a thought but was reluctant to say so. He was so interested in every phase of hospital work, and she ought to be too. "I don't know," Bonnie hedged, and wondered if he would sit with her today. That was much more important. Sometimes the boys and some of the younger interns joined the Candy Stripers, laughing and joking with them. Twice in a row, now, Nancy had come in, all pink and smiling, with Rickie Page, Jr., Dr. Page's son. He was working as cleanup boy in OR, and no job seemed too distasteful for him, Rickie, the son of the chief executive of the medical staff!

After filling his tray, David nodded pleasantly and went off to sit with the fellows. Bonnie could scarcely hide her disappointment, and was not pleased when Mavis sidled into the chair next to her.

"I see your boy friend's deserted you," she said maliciously. "You really shouldn't be so obvious, honey. I told you, play hard to get. I know that type." Before Bonnie could mke a sharp retort, Mavis added, "Oh-oh. There's the Beat of My Heart." She swept up her tray and plunked it on a nearby table where Dr. Dominic Ricci had just sat down. It looked almost accidental—but not quite.

She sure has a nerve, Bonnie thought. She shrugged her shoulders as if to throw off the annoyance she felt toward Mavis. Then she settled down to her food.

In the afternoon there was Courier Duty, and Bonnie and Mavis were thrown together again. Out of seventy-five Candy Stripers it had to be Mavis! Paula and Carol completed the quartet.

"I'm going to thaw out that Ricci if it takes all summer," Mavis vowed, settling herself on the couch.

"I'll bet you will!" Paula taunted. "What makes you think he'll stoop to cradle-snatching? I didn't see you make much progress in the cafeteria."

The afternoon dragged, with very few calls coming through, and there seemed to be no respite from the loud talk and giggling of the two "soulmates," as Bonnie had dubbed Mavis and Paula.

When a call did come in, Carol glanced at Bonnie so pleadingly that she nodded and sent her out.

"I wanted to go!" Mavis looked at Bonnie accusingly.

"No, I did. You should have let *me*, Bonnie!" Paula shrilled and poked Mavis in the ribs. A mock fight ensued immediately, and in the scuffle one of the girls kicked the door shut. "Take that!" Paula laughed loudly and threw a cushion from the couch at Mavis.

"Take it yourself!" the other girl said, flinging it back.

Bonnie was not immune to horseplay, but not in the hospital. "Stop it! Stop it, you two!" she pleaded, but the girls paid no attention. Maybe if I open the door it will have a sobering effect on these goons, she thought. She was reaching for the knob when a cushion landed smack on her head. She grabbed it. Now, if she could only catch the other one, too. As she made a grab for it and missed, the door opened and the cushion hit its mark. Bonnie turned and froze with horror.

Her cap askew, Miss Winters stood in the doorway, clutching the cushion. She was absolutely livid.

"*Well!* So this is how you amuse yourselves! Disgraceful! But I'm not surprised. It seems to me I caught you three in mischief before, only you were able to talk yourselves out of it. But not this time! Report at once to Mrs. Collins. All three of you shall be instantly dismissed. Who are *you?*" She whirled about to confront the returning Carol. "Oh, yes. Miss Kent's cousin. I suppose you, at least, can be trusted. Take over until replacements are sent to you. As for you three, march!" An irate Marine top sergeant could not have been more commanding.

The thoroughly frightened culprits slunk down the hall. Even Mavis had not recovered enough to be defiant. Bonnie put a shaking hand to her mouth. She felt as if she were going to throw up. She had no recollection of going down in the elevator, escorted by the icy Miss Winters, but there they were, marching along the first floor, with all eyes seemingly upon them. Everyone guessing that they were in terrible disgrace!

But she wasn't! She had been doing her best to stop the nonsense, Bonnie told herself, trying to take heart. She would explain and nothing would happen to her. But there was no chance to explain. Miss Winters reminded Mrs. Collins that all three were caught in the act, behaving in a most disgraceful manner, and not for the first time. They were to be dismissed at once!

Mrs. Collins' usually serene face was shocked. Bonnie thought that she looked at her longer than the others. Now was her chance to exonerate herself, if the others did not have the de-

cency to do it. But she could not make herself
speak. There was a lump in her throat, a knot
in her stomach. If she opened her mouth she
would upchuck for sure. If only this were Mrs.
Brent, she'd have a chance, but Miss Winters
stood there like an executioner, demanding
their Candy Striper lives.

Mrs. Collins was speaking, her words blurred
in Bonnie's ears. All she heard was *"Dismissed!"* like a rocket shooting through her
head. ". . . uniforms to be returned . . . a re-
flection on the Volunteer services in general.
. . ."

It was awful.

She left the hospital in a daze, walking fast, so
as to separate herself from the muttering
Mavis and the "I don't care," air of Paula. Although only a short time ago Bonnie had
thought of resigning, being dismissed was something else again.

How would she explain this at home? What
would she say to Nancy? And *David?* What
would he think of it? Miss Winters had been
angry enough in her denunciations to be over-
heard by dozens of passers-by.

"Dismissed! *Dismissed!* DISMISSED! seemed to
be shouted in a rising crescendo in her head.

ten

BONNIE HAD HOPED TO CREEP INTO THE HOUSE
unobserved but Laura shouted, "You're home
early!" as she dashed out from the back yard
to see who got off the bus, and then, in alarm,
"What's wrong, Bon? You look awful!"

She was so white and shaken that Laura
threw her arms around her sister and guided
her into the house. Upstairs in their room, Bon
nie threw herself on her bed in a torrent of
tears.

"What happened? What's the matter?" Laura
shrilled helplessly, frightened as Bonnie's weeping reached the hysterical pitch. "Shall I call

Mommy? She's at the Garden Club meeting——"

That seemed to penetrate Bonnie's grief. "No, no!" she cried, sitting up and grabbing her sister's arm. "I'm—I'll be all right."

Laura broke away, rushed into the bathroom and returned with a glass of water and a couple of aspirins. "Take these," she urged.

Bonnie gulped them down without arguing. Laura pushed her onto the bed again, put her feet up gently, and sat beside her, stroking her forehead. Bonnie's tears ran silently, leaving behind hurt hiccupy sobs.

"Do you want to tell me?" Laura asked. "Before Mommy comes home. Maybe I can help. Please, Bonnie."

Bonnie began to cry again, but in-between sobs she managed to spill out the story.

"The worms!" Laura raged indignantly. "Every time you used to mention those girls I thought they were awful. How could they let you be dismissed without saying a word for you!"

"I don't know." Bonnie put her hands over her chest as if DISMISSED were emblazoned on her crumpled pinafore. "I'm too tired to think now."

Laura continued to stroke the hot forehead until her sister fell into an exhausted sleep.

When Bonnie awakened, it was dinnertime, but she dreaded going down. How could she face Mother—and Dad? She steeled herself finally and came downstairs, with eyes still red despite repeated bathings. To her immense relief, her parents did not seem to notice anything unusual about her. She glanced at Laura and received a significant, snappy-eyed nod. Apparently her young sister had primed the family on the situation. There would be no questions for a while.

"My night to do dishes!" Laura announced after dinner, and gratefully Bonnie escaped to their room.

What would she do with herself now? Going to the Medical Center had become a part of her routine; and much more than that since she met David. She would probably never see him again, and soon tears of self-pity and indignation at the other girls were running down her cheeks again.

In the days that followed, she knew that her parents were waiting for her to speak about her dismissal, but she couldn't talk about it. She busied herself with every task she could think of. Her closet was cleaned, even Laura's hodgepodge side. Her bureau drawers were heaved out and arranged in meticulous order. When she made her bed in the morning, she caught herself turning precisely mitered hospital corners, which she promptly unmade and tucked in any old way. Anger was beginning to replace her first humiliation. She who had given freely of her time had been treated unjustly; and nobody at the Medical Center cared. Well, she hadn't really liked being a Candy Striper.

Even Nancy hadn't come over or phoned to find out exactly what had happened. She could have told her the truth. Did Nancy feel tainted by the disgrace because she had recommended her?

And there was the pink-striped uniform to return, the uniform that now had two stars. Bonnie pulled it out of the bottom drawer where she had stuffed it that awful day and stared at the stars. She had acquired the second star just the day before. Her eyes misted and she shook away the tears angrily. She didn't really care. She'd wash and iron their precious uniform and return it to them. But not the stars. She had earned them and no one could take them away from her. She ripped them off and slipped them under the handkerchiefs in the top drawer, not knowing exactly why she wanted to keep the blue stars.

As soon as the uniform was dry and ironed the next day, she packed it into a box and addressed it to the hospital. Just as she finished, Laura poked her head through the doorway.

"I have to do an errand at the Five-and-Ten for Mother. Want to come to town with me?" she asked.

Bonnie shook her head. "No, thanks. But you'll be going past the post office, so will you mail this for me?" Her voice sounded odd as she extended the box toward her sister.

"Sure!" Laura took the box, glanced at the address and lifted a stricken face. "Bonnie, you're not—you can't! Oh, Bon, surely you can do something to get back in!"

Why didn't Laura stop harping on that? Bonnie thought impatiently. Now that she was out of the Candy Stripers she was glad. The uniform was the last tie. She couldn't get rid of it fast enough. The way Laura always carried on about her hospital work! "No!" she said sharply, and turned her back on her sister.

"All right," Laura said meekly and slipped away, and Bonnie burst into tears without actually knowing why. It wasn't on account of not being a Candy Striper. It must be because she would never see David, she decided, sniffling.

Her sister remained away a long time, Bonnie thought later in the day, but when she mentioned it, Mother only said, "She'll be along soon," and went on with her work.

Bonnie pulled a book from the shelf in the living room and went out into the back yard, into the hot late July afternoon. But she could not read, and lay in the hammock with her eyes closed.

"Bonnie!" It was Nancy's soft voice.

Startled, she sat up with a jerk as Nancy said cryptically, "I thought it would take forever, but it's done now!"

Bonnie frowned, trying to understand.

"For goodness sakes, *Laura!*" Nancy called cupping her hands around her mouth, and Laura came bounding out of the house, carrying a Candy Striper's pinafore triumphantly over her arm and high-stepping like a majorette. She was wearing a smile, practically from ear to ear. As she came closer, Bonnie saw two blue stars pinned unevenly onto the bib of the pinafore.

"For you!" Laura announced, holding out the uniform. "I thought I'd never be able to find those stars in your bureau, but I did! There was no time to sew them back on, though."

"Wh-what are you talking about?" Bonnie's voice quavered.

"Nothing much, except that some people

made a mistake about my sister and now they're
sorry. Bonnie, you've been re-ah-*re-in-stat-ed!*"

"With honor!" Nancy added.

"But how? When?"

"This afternoon," Nancy said. "It seems that
when you gave Laura your uniform to mail, it
was the last straw. Instead of going to the post
office, she marched on the Hamilton Medical
Center, banners flying, and with such a right-
eous rage that she stormed past the Information
Desk before anyone knew what had happened
and flew down the corridor to Mrs. Collins'
office."

Stunned, Bonnie asked, "How did you know
where it was?"

"Floor plans," Laura said. "Studied them. Besides, her name was on the door. And boy, did I
tell her!"

Bonnie's mouth fell open. She could never
picture herself "telling" the queenly Mrs. Collins anything. "Wh-what did you say?" she
asked.

Laura grinned. "I wish you'd been there to
hear." She laid the folded striped pinafore on
her sister's lap with a flourish. "I just told her
what an awful thing had been done to you, that's
all! I said, why didn't they find out all the facts
before they put a Candy Striper out and broke
her heart."

"My heart wasn't broken."

"It was, too! I could tell. Anyway, while Mrs. Collins was still sort of gasping, another lady came in and wanted to know what it was all about. I recognized her from your description. It was Mrs. Brent! So I told her all about what happened to you and how you'd tried to stop those awful girls, Mavis and Paula—and everything." Laura paused to catch her breath. "Mrs. Brent was horrified. She said she couldn't believe you could have been involved in all that foolishness and that she was planning to check into it—only she was just back from her vacation and hadn't had time yet."

"Tell her what happened then," Nancy prompted, as if she'd heard all this before.

"Well, Mrs. Brent got right on the phone, there in Mrs. Collins' office, and called Mavis, and then she called Paula. Both of them had the decency to—to—" she glanced at Nancy for assistance.

"Exonerate Bonnie," Nancy said.

"Yes," Laura nodded. "They said you had nothing to do with all that cushion throwing. Mrs. Collins looked sort of embarrassed and sorry, but Mrs. Brent was mad. Anyway, then she called Miss Winters——"

"Oo-hh!" Bonnie shivered.

"Miss Winters took some persuading, but

finally she admitted that she might have been wrong about you and so—well, here's your uniform." She waved to it grandly and stood back to see the effect on her sister.

"The note," Nancy whispered.

"Oh, yes. Here's a note from Mrs. Brent and Mrs. Collins," Laura said, fishing for it in the pocket of her blue jeans, "asking you to come back!"

Bonnie read the somewhat crumpled note over twice and her eyes filled. Then she threw her arms around Laura and hugged her tightly. She wasn't disgraced any more! The stigma was lifted from her—thanks to the efforts of her brash little sister. "You're the best," she whispered into Laura's tumbled hair.

"Look out!" Laura said loudly, squirming away, pleased and embarrassed. "You're squashing your uniform."

"I can imagine what you've been through," Nancy said, "and I wasn't even around to help you. My married sister Louise had a baby, and I've been staying at her house, helping out. I just got back this morning myself, and happened to see Laura as she was leaving the hospital. She told me everything and I signed out and came right out with her."

A great weight seemed to lift from Bonnie. Nancy had not deserted her—and Laura, dear, blessed, impulsive, outspoken Laura had certainly proved her love and loyalty. But did she want all that Candy Striping business to start all over again? Did she want, along with the routine duties of running errands and delivering flowers, to face the tragedies and the aches and pains of total strangers? And yet, under these circumstances, what choice had she?

"You're expected back on the job at nine tomorrow," Nancy was saying. "We can go on the bus together. I've missed the work so much." She glanced at the uniform Bonnie was clutching tightly. "My, but you have been rolling up the hours. I think if you asked Mrs. Brent, she'd let you come down to the Clinic once in a while as the girls assigned there go on vacation."

Bonnie knew that to Nancy the Clinic was the highest post a Candy Striper could reach. It was also as far away as she could get from Miss Winters! And then, of course, there was David! Her heart beat a little faster as she thought of him. She would see David again! That was worth anything else she might have to face.

"All right," she told Nancy. "I'll ask about the Clinic—and—and thanks for everything."

"I only wish I were old enough!" Laura sighed. "Lucky, lucky you!"

The next day Bonnie felt like the Candy Striper Queen, herself, returning to the Center with a guard of honor. Nancy had gone with her on the bus, but at the entrance they had met Ginny Lou, Pixie and Denise, all of whom had promptly surrounded her with happy cries of welcome.

"What in the world *happened?*" Denise asked. "None of us could figure out how you'd get mixed up with that crazy Mavis and Paula, but we didn't dare call you."

"We tried to pump Carol," Pixie confessed, "but that girl's closer than a clam when she wants to be."

"She didn't really know anything about it," Bonnie said. "She came on the scene too late."

"Well, all she'd say was that she couldn't believe you had done anything with those two laughing hyenas," Pixie declared. "She even tried going to her cousin Rocheen about it, but Rocheen couldn't do anything, especially working under that awful Miss Winters."

"It's all over now, so let's not rake over the ashes," Nancy said. "Come on, or we'll all be late."

The girls filed into Mrs. Brent's office and signed in. The Director of Volunteers spoke pleasantly to all of them and asked Bonnie to remain after the others left.

"I'm dreadfully sorry about what happened," she said at once. "Injustice is awfully hard to bear, but thank goodness, we have all been set straight by that young sister of yours. I wish you could have seen her do battle for you. She was like a young Valkyrie in blue jeans! But now I think we should all go on as if nothing had happened and bear no grudges."

Bonnie thought she detected a question in that last statement. If Mrs. Brent was referring to Miss Winters, she'd better speak to *her*. It seemed to Bonnie that Miss Winters went out of her way with grudges. But she contented herself with saying merely, "Yes, Mrs. Brent. No grudges. And I am happy to be back."

"Good. Where would you like to work?"

Tentatively Bonnie mentioned the Clinic, the farthest point from Miss Winters!

Mrs. Brent glanced at her schedule of assignments. "Yes. I think they could use you in the Out Patient Department. One of the girls usually stationed with Nancy is away on vacation. I'll call and tell them you're coming. Nancy can help you get acclimated."

Bonnie found her tag, turned it over so that her name showed, and hung it on the area board in the clinic section.

Down in OPD, Nancy was waiting, ready to brief her on her duties. "Here," she said, "we get much closer to the patients than upstairs. That's why I like it. I like to deal directly with people, and we get all kinds with all sorts of injuries. First of all there are regular days on which different departments schedule cases. And then, of course, there is the emergency work at all hours of the day and night."

"I never thought of it before," Bonnie said, "but a hospital never closes its doors, does it?"

"It does not. It's always a twenty-four-hour open house here. This is the Emergency Office, and I am usually stationed here. Ambulances drive up to this entrance, and we put patients in the Receiving Room, across the way there, until it is decided whether they are to be treated in the Accident Room and released, or admitted upstairs. . . ."

"Yes, but what do *we* actually *do*?" Bonnie asked, uneasily, hoping that it wasn't too much. After all, she didn't have Nancy's passion for the work.

"Oh. Well, when someone comes in, we ask if they've been here before. If they have, we find their chart in a huge file in the records room. On this all treatments are noted. If they have not, we make out a chart." She pulled out a large card and showed it to Bonnie. "I made one out for you when you had that skinned elbow. Remember?"

Bonnie nodded. That was when David had sent her down here the day that she met him. Would she see him today? With an effort she brought her mind back to Nancy.

"We also wash instruments in the utility room," Nancy was saying. "Come, I'll show you where it is."

They turned into a doorway at the end of the hall and Nancy's voice was suddenly drowned out by a piercing shriek. Bonnie jumped violently. It sounded as if someone were being murdered right there in the utility room!

Nancy made a face and pointed to a gleaming cylindrical tank from which the horrid noise originated. "The autoclave," she shouted. "It's a sterilizing gadget for instruments. When the rubber gasket gets old there's a tiny air leak someplace and with the steam pressure up it screeches like that." She lowered her voice as she led Bonnie out.

"I wish you'd warned me," Bonnie said. "My nerves!"

"I know." Nancy laughed. "The first time I heard it I raced out of the office to see who was in such terrible agony. It gave the nurses quite a laugh. The Candy Stripers never touch the autoclave, of course, but we do get the instruments ready for it. There was nothing to wash there just now, though, so you'll have to learn about that later." She pushed a stretcher closer to the wall in the hall, and folded up a wheel chair that had been left open.

"Sometimes," she continued, "we help hold patients during treatments—youngsters mostly, who have injections, or infections lanced. Some of them have made me consider taking up the judo lessons they give at the Y! We also help in small but important ways while broken arms and legs are set. You'll learn as you go along."

Bonnie gulped. This did sound like getting close to the patient—and quite different from the work she had done upstairs. She hoped she'd be able to take it. She had never seen a broken arm or leg, before a cast had been put on, or any bad injuries from accidents, like—— She didn't want to think of particulars! Maybe this would be a quiet day, so she would get used to things gradually.

The hope was not to be realized, for even as she voiced it to herself, a car squealed to a stop at the emergency entrance and a distracted mother rushed in with a purple-faced child in her arms, gasping for breath.

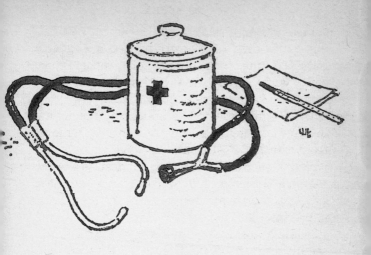

eleven

"A DOCTOR! PLEASE, A DOCTOR!" SHE PLEADED. "He's swallowed something that won't go down!"

Bonnie stared at her, confused and frightened, but Nancy was already on her feet, guiding the mother into the receiving room. "Get Miss Perkins," she said in passing, and then began to talk calmly to the mother.

Who was Miss Perkins? Bonnie ran into the hall in time to see a white uniform disappearing into the utility room. "Miss Perkins?" she called tentatively, her voice a squeak.

"Yes?" The nurse reappeared, took one

glance at Bonnie's face and raced into Receiving. From then on everything became orderly. Miss Perkins took charge of preparing the child, while Nancy raced back to the phone and summoned the house doctor. *"Stat!"*

Dr. Guthrie seemed to appear by magic, and in a few moments a large button was removed from the child's throat. He gave a lusty yell which proved that all was well, despite the fact that his throat would be sore for a few days. Medication was applied, a small fee paid, and a happy mother was on her way home.

Bonnie was limp, but Nancy returned from seeing the pair off, as if nothing extraordinary had occurred. "During most treatments you can stand in the room and watch—and if you're needed, the doctor or nurse can call you in." Then, noting Bonnie's pallor, she said, "Don't take it so hard. It's all in a day's work here. You'll get used to it. Why, we get kids who've swallowed furniture polish or cleaning fluid, or whole bottles of aspirin, and have to be pumped out, fast." She went on recounting other dire mishaps, and finished with, "Believe me, this was nothing."

Big-eyed, Bonnie couldn't quite agree with her.

The next emergency was less dramatic. A little girl was brought in with an imbedded sliver from a twig in her leg. This time Bonnie forced herself to watch while Nancy soothed the child and Dr. Celestin swiftly extracted the offending splinter. Miss Perkins came in and gave the small patient a TAT—tetanous antitoxin shot—as a precaution against possible lockjaw.

Bonnie made out the charts for the next two patients. One had an eye injury, the other an infected hand, and again forced herself to watch the treatment in both instances. The confident skill with which the work was done, the speed with which instruments were removed, and the treatment rooms set to rights, seemed to instill a calmness in her, too. These people knew exactly what they were doing, and they did it with sympathy and kindness, but not with sloppy sentimentality. She suddenly felt a little humble in their presence and almost wished that she could share their joy in their work.

She gathered up the used instruments from the next case into the small kidney-shaped emesis pan, wrapped it in the towel on which they had been laid out on a tray table, and walked out with them, just the way she had seen Nancy and Miss Perkins do. This much, at least, she could do without getting emotionally upset, she thought as she headed for the utility room. Someone would show her how to wash these things.

"Bonnie!"

She almost dropped the instruments. It was David!

"Where have you been?" he demanded. "I haven't had a glimpse of you for days."

Then he didn't know about her temporary disgrace! There was no time to explain now. "I—was away," she said. She would tell him about it later.

"You might have let a fellow know," he said reproachfully.

So he had missed her! Her heart sang. It was almost worth the disgrace to learn this.

"Well, I'm glad I caught up with you. See you home? Okay?"

"Yes." Her smile was radiant. David moved on, and she longed to turn and watch him, but controlled the impulse and stepped into the utility room.

Miss Perkins had a Monel basin of water ready in each section of the deep metal sink, which was like a small twin washtub. One basin had a disinfectant solution, and brushes nearby; the other was filled with clear water. "Not the scalpels," Miss Perkins said. Stepping away from the sterilizing autoclave she removed them quickly from the tray. "Too sharp.

I wash them myself, but it's a great help to
have the other instruments done. There's a
myringotomy set here, too. An ear infection
was opened," she explained, showing Bonnie
just how to scrub the collection of shiny surgical scissors, forceps, retractors, syringes, and
tiny, wirelike drainage tubes. Bonnie applied
herself to the task, and set out the rinsed and
wiped instruments in graduated sizes on a
towel, ready to be assembled in separate kits
and sterilized in the autoclave for re-use.

She had flinched as she rinsed the blood from
them, and the soiled gauze sponges she had dis-
carded with hasty distaste. But when Miss Perkins came in for a moment and praised her for
the neat array of sparkling clean instruments
she felt an unexpected wave of pride and pleasure in a job well done.

"Wash and wipe your hands thoroughly
each time," Miss Perkins advised before she
left. "And be sure to put on some of this cream
solution," she added, handing Bonnie a bottle,
"otherwise your skin will get chapped In our
work we're forever washing our hands with
strong solutions."

She had treated Bonnie like a mature fellow
worker, a responsible person, even though she
was new to the department. Petite, dark-haired

Miss Perkins wasn't a bit like that cold-hearted Miss Winters!

Bonnie finished her first day in OPD tired but happy. She had learned so much—not deftness, as yet, nor complete ease with patients, which Nancy had—but she felt that she had made a start in the right direction. And that nice Miss Perkins had actually thanked her "for helping out." She'd have a lot to tell the family today. Bonnie smiled and held herself straighter as she walked out of the Medical Center, feeling more important than she had for days.

And there was David, waiting for her in his ancient "half-convertible." She was so happy that she had difficulty restraining her impulse to fly.

All at once Bonnie was glad that she wasn't Rock Caldwell's steady because the way she felt about David, she couldn't be, possibly. She still liked Rock, of course. As a friend. And he hadn't forgotten her. There had been three postcards from him, demanding letters; she had written him twice.

"Come, your ladyship!" David held the car door open for her and Bonnie stepped in gladly.

They did not stop talking all the way home. Or rather, David talked—of the importance of

hospitals to communities, of his own hopes in
the administration field. She listened, charmed
by his voice, his words, his sincerity and ambi-
tion.

As they pulled up in front of her house
David placed his hand over hers. "You're
awfully nice to talk to, Star Girl."

Bonnie was so moved, she couldn't answer.

Walking up to the house, after he drove
away, she decided to ask Mother about having
David over for dinner some day. Her parents
had expressed a desire to meet him, and he
would probably appreciate having some home
atmosphere for a change. Also, it would be a
graceful way to get to know him better. Or
should she wait until he asked her for a date
first? She didn't want David to think she was
chasing him!

Her dream about David was interrupted by
Laura who demanded to know everything that
had happened at the Center. "Aren't you glad
you're back?" she asked.

"Yes," Bonnie said, but she was thinking of
David.

"I knew you'd be! Where did you work
today?" Laura wanted to know and almost
swooned with envy when she heard about the
OPD. Her appetite for clinical details was in-
satiable.

"That reminds me," Bonnie said, "you keep out of the way when Nancy's brothers are on the lawn practicing fly casting. We had a little girl with a fish hook in her hand." She shuddered, remembering the injury.

"You sounded just like Mother, then. What did it look like?"

"Not very nice—and very painful. One of her brothers hooked her."

"How did they get it out? Did you see?"

Bonnie nodded. It hadn't been very pleasant. She could still hear the child's screams in her ears when she thought about it. "Of course a local anesthetic deadened the pain," she told Laura, "but the only way to get a fish hook out is to push it through and then clip the end. Luckily it had only one prong."

After dinner she told her parents about her day. Although Mother would not allow clinical details to float around the table, she was becoming increasingly interested in her hospital accounts, Bonnie noticed, and she did not seem to worry about germs as much. Father's interest was very quiet, and she caught him watching her steadily at times. Both of them seemed very happy to have her reinstated—vindicated. They had been very sweet during those difficult days of her disgrace and she was overwhelmed with a sudden extra fondness for both of them.

"Come on out for a game of badminton bebore it gets too dark," Laura urged, breaking in on the mood. "I've been practicing with Dodie so maybe I can beat you now, especially since you haven't had Rock around to keep up your form."

"All right, get the rackets and the birds," Bonnie said, "while I slip into my shorts."

It was a lovely, still evening, and not too hot. Just right for a game, Bonnie thought, and wondered if David played badminton. She must remember to ask him. It would give them something to do together.

"Ready?" Laura called, and launched into a fast game. She had been practicing, Bonnie discovered at once, as her younger sister kept her running all over the court. But Laura finally made a mistake by sending over a high soaring bird. Bonnie waited for it to come down and then smashed it over, close to the net for a winning point.

"Hey!" Laura shouted as Bonnie was about to collapse on the grass. "There's Cliff! Hi, Cliff! Come on over and play with us."

Bonnie turned and saw their next-door neighbor shaking his head. "Sorry, I'm busy," he said, and loped back into the house. The

stuck-up thing, Bonnie thought. Positively anti-
social. A month ago she might have cared, but
not now. Still, Cliff's absolute indifference ran-
kled.

"Oh, well——" Laura flopped on the grass,
stomach down and propped up her chin with
her hands. "I tried. I hate to see you without
dates just because Rock's not here; and with a
perfectly good boy next door going to waste."

"Laura Schuyler, I'll thank you not to try
to fix me up with dates!" Bonnie was indignant.
"I can go out any time I want. In fact, Pixie is
having a pajama party next week and——"

"Oh, hen parties," Laura shrugged. "I was
talking about *dates.*"

"Well, you may be surprised one of these
days," Bonnie told her—and would say nothing
more, no matter how Laura teased. With David
in the offing, what did she care about Cliff Coburn or anybody else for that matter. David
was very special.

She was scheduled in Pediatrics the next
morning, the first day she had spent any length
of time in that department. As soon as she arrived on the floor, Miss McNeil, the nurse in
charge, directed her to a child who needed
extra watching.

"Peter had an emergency eye operation last

night and he's quite miserable," she said as she led Bonnie into the glass-walled room.

Peter was about seven years old. His face was flushed, one eye had a wad of cotton taped over it, the other had a small wire basket held in place with more tape. His right arm was held straight inside a round cardboard carton so he could not bend his elbow and touch his face, but his left arm was free. A practical nurse was sitting beside him, reading from a picture book and keeping a firm control over his wandering left arm, each time Peter reached for his face.

As soon as Bonnie came in, the nurse handed her the picture book and hurried away to other duties.

"Peter," the head nurse said, "this is Bonnie. She's going to stay and read to you until your mother comes. You'll be a good boy, won't you?"

"Ummm," Peter mumbled. "Thirsty. . . ."

Miss McNeil pointed to a glass of water with a bent straw in it. "Give him a sip now and then," she directed, "but above all, keep him quiet and don't let him get at that wire basket over his eye."

Nervously Bonnie settled herself on the high stool beside Peter's bed. What had happened to his eyes? What if he managed to elude her and get at that protecting basket with his free hand? But when she began to read, patting his arm gently, the little boy seemed to relax. She made her voice soft and light, and explained the pictures that went with the text. Peter seemed to listen and forget about tossing on his high-sided bed.

In the second bed there was another little boy who watched her with big, unhappy eyes. While she read to Peter, two doctors came in and began to examine Bruce. After the doctors left, Bonnie turned toward him occasionally and tried to give him a reassuring smile. Poor little fellow—what a strange new world this must be for him.

By the time Peter was asleep his mother arrived. "Thank you for taking care of him," she said gratefully. "It was so sudden. So awful. He was playing with his little sister. All of a sudden she picked up a belt and swung it around—and—and the buckle hit Peter full in the eye. H-he may lose it." She wiped away a tear and Bonnie felt like crying right along with her. Poor, poor little Peter. Why did things like this have to happen!

She said something consoling to her, then turned to Bruce and somehow put on a cheerful face for him. He, too, needed help. Miss McNeil looked in and smiled at her.

"Good girl," she said. "Try to cheer him up. He's that scared of the operation. He'll be going up in a little while."

She came back shortly with a hypodermic, and Bruce gave a lusty, *"Ow!"* as the needle found its mark. Bonnie read and talked to him until he fell asleep from the sedation. She slipped out of the room, just as two nurses came in to take Bruce, bed and all to the operating suite. Directly after his operation he would be put back into his own bed in the Recovery Room, and once he had regained consciousness, he would be wheeled back into Pediatrics.

Everything was certainly orderly and systematic in a hospital, Bonnie thought. If only there wasn't so much pain and human emotion involved.

It was eleven o'clock now, and time for the children to have lunch. "Will you help feed a little one out in the solarium?" Miss McNeil asked, pausing in a rapid dash in the opposite direction. "Sally is a long-term patient here She's been in and out with leg operations. She's a bit slow up here," Miss McNeil tapped her forehead, "but a dear sweet thing. You'll need a bit of patience, though." She breezed away, leaving Bonnie to think this over.

At least Sally wasn't one of the really sick

ones if she was in the solarium that had been fixed up as a playroom for the young patients.

There were three children in the lovely sunroom: two little boys and Sally, each about five or six years old. They were seated in low chairs with their lunch trays on small tables before them. The little boys were eating slowly and methodically, but Sally only stared at her food and occasionally slapped the back of her spoon into the mashed potatoes.

"Hello, Sally," Bonnie said cheerfully. "M'mm, what a delicious lunch."

The little girl tilted her head and scowled. Bonnie pulled up a low bench and sat down beside her. Sally twisted away, extending her bandaged leg as she did so. "Don't hurt me," she said plaintively, and Bonnie felt a stab of pain for the child.

"I'm here to help you eat your lunch," she said quietly. "Here, let's have some. It smells so good." She tried to recall how she had once coaxed Laura when she'd been ill. It didn't work on Sally, though. She opened her mouth, but as the spoon came close, she clamped her lips tightly. It wasn't long before Bonnie was completely frustrated, and what was worse, the little boys who had been eating so well now stopped operations and watched her and Sally with interest. It must be quite a show, Bonnie thought. She wasn't getting anywhere, and Sally's lunch was getting cold.

The next time Bonnie brought the spoon over, Sally ducked away, scooped up a Panda from the floor and sat clutching it in front of her. Inspired, Bonnie extended the spoon toward the Panda, pretended to feed it, and said, "That's a good Panda." Then, although Sally expected the next mouthful to be for her, Bonnie jumped up, thrust a toy into the hands of each of the little boys and "fed" the toys a bit of their dinner. She then popped a spoonful into the boys' surprised little mouths—while Sally watched—no longer the center of attention.

By the time Bonnie returned to Sally and started to "feed" the Panda again, Sally's mouth was all ready and she pulled Bonnie's hand over toward it. From then on she didn't have a bit of trouble with Sally, except that the little boys thought the game was great fun, so occasionally, while Sally was chewing, Bonnie jumped up and fed each of them in turn. The children's open mouths made her think of the nestful of hungry robins outside her bedroom window.

Miss McNeil, hearing the jolly laughter in the sunroom, peeked in and congratulated Bonnie with a broad smile. It made her feel like a general, with a situation well in hand.

Nevertheless, when her own lunchtime came, she wasn't a bit sorry and, with a sigh of relief, joined Nancy and a group of other Candy Stripers seated at a long table.

twelve

"WHEW!" NANCY SAID, "WHAT A MORNING WE
had in the clinic. I think every other child in
Hamilton managed either to break an arm, leg,
collarbone, or swallow something he shouldn't
have."

"My goodncool" Pixie was awed. "What did
you do for them?"

"Which ones?" Nancy asked.

"The ones who swallowed things," Pixie
said.

"I don't think I'd better tell you during
lunch, though I've gotten so it doesn't bother

me any more—clinical details like stomach
pumps, I mean."

Bonnie glanced at Nancy curiously. Would
she get that way after a while? Nancy certainly
did not seem to suffer agonies with every patient the way she did. But perhaps Nancy was
another type of person.

"All right, tell me afterward, then," Pixie
said. "I had two darling old ladies to amuse
this morning. They were both in the solarium
on Fifth and they both loved Thackeray, so I
read from *Vanity Fair* to them. They made
me promise to come back this afternoon.
I'm going to be so literary by the time school
begins, my English teacher won't know me!
What did you do, Bon?"

So Bonnie told them about Pediatrics and
how she'd gotten around the stubborn Sally.

"You're a genius!" Pixie said. "I think I'd
have been tempted to whop her. Not really, of
course," she added hastily. "Just mentally, sort
of."

"Don't think I wasn't," Bonnie confessed. I
guess I inherited Sally today because this is
Ginny Lou's day off, and I think Carol is off,
too. Those two are usually in Pediatrics, but I
don't think I could stand too much of it. All
that wailing, and the oxygen tents where the
kids lie so quietly."

In the afternoon she was assigned to the surgical patients on Second. There were a great many errands to do, and many flowers to deliver. The patients were pleased when she called them by name. When she worked on the same floor the next day, the patients, too, seemed to recognize her as she made her rounds. There were new people in two beds, though. Mr. Harris and Mrs. Ainsley were no longer on this floor; she hoped they had been transferred.

That night, after her father was through with the *Hamilton Daily*, Bonnie leafed through it and paused at a section she had never found of interest before. Walking behind her chair, Father glanced over her shoulder and stopped short.

"Why in the world are you reading the obituary column?" he asked.

"Well," Bonnie explained, "I'm getting to know a lot of patients at the Center and today I missed two, so I thought, well, you know."

"And were they?" her father asked gently.

"No." Bonnie sounded relieved. "Their names weren't mentioned. I think they were moved to another floor. Anyway, they were looking very healthy. They may even have been discharged."

"You are getting caught up in your work, aren't you?"

"In a way," Bonnie answered honestly. "But I think I'm overly sympathetic."

Mother walked in on the tail end of their conversation. "No fair if you've been telling your father about your day," she said. "I want to hear about it, too. In fact, since you spent last evening with Pixie Chase, I have two days to catch up on."

Bonnie was still carefully deleting from her accounts anything that might upset her mother, so she left out the little boy with the eye operation, but she did tell her about cheering Bruce before his appendectomy, and then gave a detailed account of how she'd managed to coax Sally into eating her lunch.

Her father smiled, but her mother's forehead furrowed and she said, "The poor little thing. She sounds as if she needed mothering. I guess it's this sort of thing that Pat Wheeler meant when she told me how valuable volunteers are in the hospital." She seemed very thoughtful as she took out her mending basket.

The telephone rang and Bonnie's heart skipped. Could it be David? She had not seen him for two days. Perhaps he had missed her and——

"It's Pixie, for you!" Laura called from the hallway, and Bonnie's heart settled into its normal beat. Pixie was probably calling her about that pajama party.

"Hello," she said, trying not to sound disappointed. Why didn't David think to call her?

The phone rang again immediately after she hung up, and Bonnie picked it up, thinking that Pixie had forgotten to tell her something. But it was David this time!

"Just wanted to know how you're getting along," he said, while Bonnie listened blissfully. "I've been helping move old medical records in the nether regions, far and away from the rest of humanity," he explained. "I think I'll be there for the balance of the week."

They talked for about five minutes, and what they said was inconsequential, but the fact that David had called her spoke volumes to Bonnie. He did not ask for a date, but he did miss her when he did not see her, and for the present that was enough. Maybe next time . . .

Bonnie awakened to a glorious sunny morning the next day. All was right with her world because last night David had phoned her. In the twin bed next to hers, Laura was sleeping, her blonde hair tumbled. It was getting longish and a home permanent was indicated in the near future, Bonnie thought. They'd have to plan for it some week end soon.

"Wake up, sleepyhead, or all the early worms will be gone," she said, reaching over to shake a chubby arm.

"Ugh," Laura muttered. "Mentioning worms at this hour."

"Look who's talking! The girl I had to persuade not to keep pet mice in our room!"

"Maybe I'm growing up," Laura said, sitting up and yawning like Mammoth Cave. "It's a sign. I read about it. Sen-ti-sivity."

"You mean, *sensitivity*, goopus!" Bonnie jumped out of bed, ran to the window and surveyed the world, and then pirouetted toward the bathroom, singing, *"O, what a beautiful morning!"*

"I know what that's a sign of, too!" Laura called after her. "Love! Your face could have lit up the whole neighborhood after that second phone call last night. It's that boy at the hospital, I'll bet. No wonder you haven't been interested in Cliff."

Bonnie paused in mid-step. She didn't quite put a name on her feeling for David, but Laura had. Was she in love with him? She wasn't really sure, she thought, as she stepped into the bathroom. Not yet.

Washed, and dressed in her uniform, Bonnie went downstairs to help with breakfast. The small kitchen radio was on and her mother, looking distressed, was listening to the eight-o'clock news on the local station.

"Oh, Bonnie," she said, "there was a terrible fire last night at Fairhills. That's the new community north of here. A young mother was burned to death and the father just barely managed to save their baby before he collapsed. They were taken to the Medical Center. What a sad thing to happen."

"Yes," Bonnie agreed, pityingly. Of all injuries, burns were the worst, she'd heard. She studied her mother curiously. Lately she had been bringing all sorts of items pertaining to the Center to Bonnie's attention and asking a great many questions about her work there. It was getting so that she no longer had to give one account to Laura and a strictly censored one to Mother, and that was a relief. She didn't really want to live her day over twice. Then there was David—if it weren't for him, she would be tempted to curtail her hours at the Center. It wasn't, of course that there weren't bright spots in the day. There were. Lots of them. People getting well, rejoining their families, mothers going home proudly with brand-new babies. But there was the other side, too, to which she did not think she would ever adjust.

And yet, by the time she reached the hospital

doors, Bonnie had begun speculating about these burned people from Fairhills. The father was probably on Fourth—in the Quiet Room behind the nurse's station, if he was critically injured; and the baby in the East Wing, in Pediatrics. Thank goodness Nellie Belle was there, too. If anyone could ease the pain for the poor little mite, the kindly colored practical nurse would. She was always assigned to such cases.

"Bonnie," Mrs. Brent said when she was signing in, "you may go down to the Clinic in the afternoon, but will you help out on Fourth this morning?"

Her pencil faltered. Fourth! The unpleasant Miss Winters' domain. Was Mrs. Brent testing her out? "I'll be glad to," she said, keeping her face expressionless.

Making empty beds, fetching and carrying nourishment trays, arranging flowers, answering patients' signals, and wheeling patients to their treatments was routine for her now—except under Miss Winters' critical eye. The elderly nurse gave Bonnie a cool nod when she came on the floor, but Miss Kent smiled at her warmly.

Bonnie wasn't on the floor long before she discovered that she had been right about the burned man. Mr. Martin was in the Quiet

Room, swathed in bandages from head to foot
and kept under sedation so that he would not
move or ask questions. Poor fellow, Bonnie
thought, walking away from his room fast. And
the baby, how badly was the baby hurt?

When her dities were over, she could not
bring herself to go to lunch without finding out.
She slipped into Pediatrics just as a red-eyed
Ginny Lou dashed into the nurses' lavatory.
Bonnie followed. Ginny Lou was bent over a
basin, splashing water on her face.

"What's the matter?" Bonnie asked, never
having seen her friend upset before.

"Wendy," Ginny Lou murmured, a catch in
her throat. "That poor little thing."

"The Martin Baby?" Bonnie guessed.

Ginny nodded. "Only seven months old—and
—and this happens."

"Is Nellie Belle with her?"

"No. Nellie Belle's off today. They tried to get
her, but she's away, visiting her sister out of
town someplace—and that baby just cries and
cries. It's heartbreaking. She's asleep now. I've
been with her all morning."

Bonnie put her arms around Ginny Lou and
the other girl turned and wept into her shoulder. But the tears did not last long. Ginny Lou
pulled herself together, and Bonnie found herself returning to Wendy's room with her.

The tiny baby, swathed in bandages, with nothing but her small mouth visible, shook her. Bonnie clasped her hands tightly. No wonder Ginny had gone to pieces.

"We have a number of very sick kids here," Ginny Lou whispered, "and several postoperative cases which have to be watched closely. Wendy isn't critical so a nurse can't be assigned to her all the time and I took her over. I hope she'll sleep a while. Being so little, I guess they can't give her too many sedatives; and when she's awake she cries."

In her small high crib, Wendy moved convulsively. The little mouth opened and a plaintive wail began. Ginny Lou's fingers tightened on the crib side.

"I'll stay with you," Bonnie said impulsively.

"Will you?" Ginny Lou was almost pathetically grateful.

Bonnie moved to the far side of the crib and lowered the railing. "There, there," she said softly. "Wendy is all right. Wendy is a good girl. There, there, darling. There, there sweetheart." Her fingers, feather light, patted the baby's shoulder. The tiny wail ceased, and Wendy relaxed.

"You're a genius," Ginny Lou whispered. "You have a magic touch, like Nellie Belle."

Bonnie looked up in surprise. Of course what

Ginny said wasn't true. It was just that she had
observed Nellie Belle care for small patients in
this way.

For the rest of the day the girls hovered
over Wendy Martin, taking turns in comforting her, under Miss McNeil's supervising eye.
Bonnie tried to recall all the lullabies she knew,
and when she ran out of those, she sang old-
time ballads she had learned from her mother
and father. Her voice was low and sweet, and
the baby seemed to respond to its soothing quality. Nellie Belle almost always sang to her patients, Bonnie recalled. Perhaps Wendy's poor
mother had also sung to her baby. Sometimes it
was hard to keep back tears, and then the patting and, "There, there," was resumed, but between them the girls managed to keep a con-
stant vigil over the child.

By the middle of the afternoon Bonnie was
tired, and someone brought over a high stool
and put it under her. Her head throbbed and
her eyes felt hot and dry, but Wendy had
hardly cried at all. Doctors and nurses came
and went, going about their skilled duties of
medication, feeding, changing, but it was
Bonnie's singing and Ginny Lou's soft talk that
soothed the child.

Bonnie's neck hurt and her back seemed set
in a painful curve over the crib, and on the

other side was Ginny Lou, white and trembling.

"Go off for a while," Bonnie advised, and gratefully Ginny Lou slipped away.

As Bonnie sat alone, crooning a wordless song, she felt strong, yet gentle hands lifting her away from the crib. "Go home, child. You look plumb wore out. You've done your job and Nellie Belle's here now."

"Oh-h, Nellie Belle!" Bonnie could have fallen on that ample bosom and wept.

"There, there." The timeless words of comfort came from someone on the other side of her. It was Mrs. Brent, with eyes glistening. "I'm so proud of you girls, I'd like to shout it from the housetops," she said. "Instinctively, you two gave that baby what she needed most during these hours—TLC—tender, loving care." She hugged Bonnie to her. "I couldn't imagine what had become of you when you didn't report in at the Clinic, until Dr. Guthrie phoned down to tell me what you girls were doing."

Bonnie's hands flew to her mouth. "I forgot all about the Clinic," she cried guiltily.

"They managed," Mrs. Brent said dryly. "Anyway, Dr. Guthrie issued orders that you girls were to be left alone with Wendy until

Nellie Belle could be recalled. You were doing precisely what was needed."

Nellie Belle was already settled on the stool vacated by Bonnie, half-murmuring, half-humming in her rich low voice.

Mrs. Brent led Bonnie away. "Judging by the rumblings in your tummy, the Clinic was not the only thing you forgot. Did you have lunch?"

"Lunch?" Bonnie repeated vaguely, and all at once felt famished.

"As I thought. Oh, you precious girls. Your enthusiasm and devotion are positively awe-inspiring," Mrs. Brent said.

Bonnie squirmed uncomfortably. Mrs. Brent didn't know it, but she was speaking to one of the least devoted. Why did everyone assume that she was mad about this work? She wasn't. She was merely finishing a job she had undertaken—much too lightheartedly and impulsively. Whatever else this summer might teach her, one thing Bonnie would never do was jump into anything again! At this moment she was so tired she could have pushed one of the patients out and crawled into bed. Thank goodness Mrs. Brent, with her ideals and dreams, wasn't a mind reader.

"Come in here for a quick pickup of energy," Mrs. Brent said, guiding Bonnie into a floor kitchen. There she produced a glass of orange juice and followed this up with milk and cookies. "This should hold you until you get home for dinner."

"M'mmm'mmm," Bonnie mumbled, gobbling away. "Where's Ginny Lou?"

"She was sent home with one of our social workers. I'll take you home myself. I'm leaving for the day now."

While waiting for Mrs. Brent to close her office in the administration wing, Bonnie saw Miss Winters approaching from the opposite end of the hall.

"Going home at long last, Bonnie?" Miss Winters asked. "You did a good day's work."

She passed on, leaving Bonnie gaping. Miss Winters had actually smiled at her—well, almost! Had she decided that Candy Stripers had some use around the hospital after all?

Further speculation was cut off by Mrs. Brent's reappearance. The Director of Volunteers always walked at a brisk pace, and it made Bonnie think that she was running as she tried to keep up.

Settled in the car, Bonnie leaned back against the seat and closed her eyes.

"We have a surprise for the Candy Stripers next week," Mrs. Brent said. "A picnic-swim next Thursday on the Warren Tilford estate. You know the big chemical plant at the edge of town? Mr. Tilford owns it, and he and his wife are tremendously interested in the Medical Center and everything that goes on there. They often open their home and grounds for our social or fund-raising functions. The picnic-swim has become an annual affair. Well, aren't you pleased?"

Bonnie was too tired to think very clearly. "Next Thursday I'll have my third hundred hours. My third star," she blurted.

Mrs. Brent burst into laughter. "You girls amaze me constantly. You'd work twenty-four hours a day, if we let you, every day of the week."

Again Mrs. Brent misunderstood. Bonnie had been merely totaling up her hours—rather fuzzily—and the words had slipped out. The stars were a sign of achievement, of course, but when she was through at the Center, come September, she would remove them from her uniform and mount them prominently in her room as a reminder to look carefully before she leaped. But Mrs. Brent insisted on attributing Worthy Thoughts to her.

"Third star or not," Mrs. Brent went on, "I'm going to insist that you go on this picnic. But to make up for the terribleness of it, I'm going to invite some boys to go along. Rickie Page, David Adams, and some of the other young men we have working at the center. Ah!" She saw that Bonnie's interest was caught. "I thought that would make a difference. Imagine having to *bribe* people to go on a picnic!"

This time Bonnie laughed, too. There were some compensations to her work at the hospital after all!

Mrs. Brent deposited her in front of the Schuyler house and drove away with a friendly wave of the hand and a shake of her shapely head. And Bonnie almost wished she were really the ideal Candy Striper the Director of Volunteers imagined her to be.

But a picnic-swim—with David! It would be like having a date with him. Hurry up, Thursday, she thought, with renewed vigor.

thirteen

WALKING UP THE HOSPITAL DRIVE THE NEXT morning Bonnie fell in step with Pixie, her pony tail bobbing saucily.

"Hi!" Pixie said. "Where are you going to be today?"

"I'm a sort of floater," Bonnie replied. "Mrs. Brent sends me wherever a Candy Striper is needed, so I never know ahead of time. I like to work in different areas."

"I've been asking for duty on Second. The surgical patients are interesting—and that awesome Miss Winters isn't there! The last time I was on Fourth I absent-mindedly threw the

179

rubber sheet from the bed I was changing
down the laundry chute."

"Oh, my! Did she find out?"

"Did she! She was right behind me when I
did it. You should have heard her lecture on
irresponsibility. Then she sent me to the Laundry to retrieve the darned thing."

"You mean you had to dig through all that
soiled linen?" Bonnie asked distastefully.

"No." Pixie's pony tail flew from side to side.
"A tiny Chinese came running the minute I got
off the elevator. Miss Winters must have
phoned down to him. He practically pushed
me out of the way and dived into the soiled
linen bins, chattering like an angry chipmunk.
'Allatime gels do stupid thing. Allatime thlow
thing down. Lubbel sheets, instlumens. Tch-
tch-tch . . . Hele is. Go 'way now. Don' come
back. Goo-by.' "

Pixie's imitation of the angry little man was
so hilarious that Bonnie doubled up with laughter. "You must tell this at your pajama party
tomorrow," she gasped. "At least that doesn't
sound as if you were the only one who did such
things."

"That's true." Pixie looked mollified. "Besides, did you hear of the student nurse who
got so rattled she almost emptied a you-know-
what down one of the chutes?"

"No!" Bonnie was horrified.

"Yes. And guess where? On Fourth, naturally. That Winters woman is enough to rattle anybody. Miss Kent grabbed the student in the nick of time."

"Bonnie, will you work on Second with Pixie?" Mrs. Brent asked, her pencil poised over her schedule sheet as the girls signed in.

"I'll be glad to." Bonnie made the standard little speech automatically now. Volunteers were supposed to be "glad" to do anything asked of them. She turned over her tag on the Second Floor section, and with a swish of starched skirts, the girls hurried to the elevators.

"There are several accident cases up there," Pixie said. "Wait till you see 'em. A young fellow with his jaw all wired up, a broken leg, and an eye he almost lost. He fell asleep at the wheel of his car."

Bonnie shuddered.

"Then there's a girl who fell with her horse. Ankle crushed, but luckily nothing more. And a young woman with both arms broken. Another auto accident victim."

The girls reported at the Nurse's Station and found that Miss Kent was substituting for the head nurse, who was on vacation. Both

Miss Kent and the floor secretary smiled with relief when they saw the Candy Stripers. "Are we glad to have you!" the secretary said. "Pixie will you take these slips to their destinations? You know, Lab, X-ray, Diet Kitchen, Information, and so on." And, as Pixie vanished, "Bonnie, there are four boxes of flowers in the utility room. Will you take them around to the patients and then arrange them?"

"I'll be glad to!" Bonnie swung away. Taking flowers around was fun. The patients were always pleased to get them, and she liked to make arrangements.

One of the bouquets was for Mrs. Ellen Howard, the young woman with the broken arms. She was so depressed by her accident that not even the sight of the gladiolas cheered her. Bonnie did her best with the tall pink and white spikes and bore the arrangement proudly down the hall.

"Aren't they lovely, Mrs. Howard?" she asked. "Shall I put them on your dresser here where you can see them?"

"Yes, do," Mrs. Howard replied indifferently. "Maybe they'll block out the mirrors so I won't keep thinking of how I must look."

Bonnie glanced around. A tear was coursing down the young woman's cheek.

"I was on my way to have my hair done.

Get the whole works at the beauty parlor, when this happened," Mrs. Howard murmured.

"I'm so sorry," Bonnie told her. "But you are lucky. These accidents can be so much worse."

"I know." Ellen Howard took hold of herself. "I keep telling myself that. Only I'm so helpless with my arms in these horrid casts. I can't do a thing for myself. Not even comb my hair. I must be a sight. Hold up that hand mirror for me, will you?"

Bonnie hesitated, wishing the conversation had taken another tack. Mrs. Howard was definitely not at her best. Her hair was lanky, there was no make-up on her face. "Maybe I could fix you up a bit," she offered impulsively. "Would you like me to?"

A hopeful gleam came into the young woman's eyes. "Would I! My husband's coming in on leave tonight. He's with the Air Force in England I haven't seen him for almost a year."

"I'll ask the nurse," Bonnie said, whisking out. Surely she could not harm the patient by applying a little make-up and combing her hair. It would do her morale a world of good.

Miss Kent agreed. "To quote one of my teachers," she added, "it is the whole patient who requires attention, mentally and physically—not only an arm or a leg. We are not bolt

fasteners on a medical assembly line. Go ahead,
Bonnie."

Beaming, Bonnie hurried off to find the necessary toilet articles in the dresser drawer
and Mrs. Howard's face glowed as Bonnie applied powder and lipstick. "I'll brush your
hair, too," she said. "You let me know if I hurt
you. Maybe we could fluff it out a bit."

"All right. But I'm afraid it will only tangle.
That's why they slick it back like this when I get
my morning bath."

A few flicks of brush and comb, and Ellen
Howard looked a great deal better. Bonnie held
a mirror up to her. Mrs. Howard smiled her
thanks. "At least now I don't look an absolute
fright, but I wish I could do something about
my hair."

"Why not cut it?" Bonnie asked. "One of
those cute French hair-do's?"

"No. It's too straight and I'd look as if I'd got
caught in a lawnmower. I wish I could get it
waved," Mrs. Howard said wistfully.

Bonnie pondered that. Mrs. Howard would
look sweet with short curls and most home
permanents were simple affairs. She and Laura
gave them to each other—in fact, Laura was
due for a new one. But how to give a permanent to a patient flat on her back? "Excuse me,"
Bonnie said, and slipped out of the room. She

would consult Miss Kent before getting Mrs. Howard excited.

"Oh, dear," Miss Kent said. "I really don't know——"

"But her husband is coming from England. They haven't seen each other for months. He's Air Force," Bonnie pleaded. "This is so special, and she wants to look her best."

"It's such an ambitious project for you to tackle."

"Pixie will help me," Bonnie urged. "Besides, didn't you say it's the whole patient who requires attention?"

Miss Kent weakened. "I suppose it could be managed in the treatment room. The table is adjustable—and they do have quick waves where prior washing of the hair isn't even necessary." She was thinking out loud. "All right, I'll consult Mrs. Howard's doctor. He'll probably think I'm mad, but maybe he'll go along with us."

The doctor roared at the idea. He said it was preposterous! The vanity of women but go ahead. Such things sometimes brought unexpected therapeutic results, and he had noted how depressed Mrs. Howard was.

Miss Kent hung up the telephone with a trembling hand but triumph in her eye. "The 'whole patient' won," she said. "We'll call a couple of orderlies to help move Mrs. Howard and I'll fix up the treatment table. You go and tell her about it. I'll phone a drugstore in town and have them deliver the easiest waving set they have."

Bonnie could have kissed Miss Kent.

A short time later she and Pixie, supervised by the nurse, proceeded with the assurance of professional hairdressers. An hour and a half after they started, Mrs. Howard was back in her bed, her short-cropped hair neatly rolled into pin curls, and a smile of pure bliss on her lips as she fell into her first happy sleep since her accident.

Bonnie and Pixie cleaned up the treatment room and hurried away for a late lunch.

"Do you feel like the Good Fairy?" Pixie asked in the elevator, her voice subdued and a little surprised.

"Something like it, I guess," Bonnie replied. "Anyway, I feel awfully good inside. I promised Mrs. Howard to come up before I go off for the day and comb out her pin curls and freshen her make-up. She'll look pretty as a bride for that husband of hers. They were married only two weeks when he went in the Service."

"M'mm," Pixie murmured sympathetically. Of late she wasn't as ready with quips and pranks, Bonnie thought, glancing at her friend's thin, serious face.

"Y'know," Pixie said, her brow furrowed, "I feel lots older. In just these few weeks I've been at the Center, I feel as if I'd lived years."

"Come to think of it, so do I," Bonnie confessed.

"I guess that's because this is such a grown-up world, full of problems that never entered our heads before. My mother's beginning to notice!" Some of the old Pixie sparkle returned.

"I hope the improvement's been gradual," Bonnie teased. "We wouldn't want your mother to go into shock."

It was late, the Cafeteria was quite empty, and by this time there wasn't much choice of menu. The girls selected sandwiches, a salad and milk and settled themselves at a table near a window. A student nurse came in, chose some food and stood uncertainly at the edge of the cafeteria rail, looking lonesome.

Bonnie and Pixie exchanged a glance and both beckoned to her simultaneously. The girl hurried over.

"Thanks for taking me in," she said. "I hate to eat alone, and outside of my classmates, I don't know anybody here. My name's Sara Foster."

The girls introduced themselves and for a while they all ate in companionable silence, and then Sara's nostrils twitched. "Did either of you have a permanent today?" she asked.

"No, but we gave one," Pixie said. "Do we still smell of the lotion?"

"Probably to no one else but me," Sara said ruefully. "I have an extraordinary sense of smell. It's kind of a curse, really, because coupled with it is a very low tolerance for certain odors, like ether and formaldehyde and disinfectants."

"You poor thing!" Bonnie was sympathetic. "How do you stand training?"

"Through sheer will power," Sara confessed. "I pray constantly that I'll get through all right, because once I'm graduated, I can find a job where such smells will be at a minimum."

"Why did you ever decide to take up nursing?" Bonnie asked.

"I thought I'd like it. I'm afraid I came into it harboring a great many delusions as to how romantic it is." Sara made a face. "That's one thing you kids won't do. Being Candy Stripers you have a pretty good idea right now of what nursing is like."

Yes, Bonnie thought, and wished she'd known what Candy Striping was like before she'd volunteered! Except, of course, she wouldn't have met David then.

"You mean, now that you've started your schooling, you don't like nursing?" Pixie's eyes were big.

"No, not that," Sara said. "But nothing in my previous experience had prepared me for it, and all the books I'd read had painted too romantic a picture. We didn't have anything like junior aides at the hospital in the small town from which I came. If we'd had, I'd have joined the group, and then I might have learned a few things, like taking Italian or Spanish or German, instead of French along with my Latin. I have never had occasion to use French. I don't think anyone would understand me if I did. But the girls who have studied other languages manage to understand our foreign patients. Say, whom did you give that permanent wave to?" Sara asked, suddenly backtracking.

They told her about Mrs. Howard and her Air Force husband.

Sara looked from one to the other admiringly. "That was a nice thing to do. There's a lot more to nursing than healing people's bodies. Look, I'm going to be on Second early this evening, I'll look out for your Mrs. Howard."

"Fine!" Bonnie was relieved. "When I take

care of some of these people, I get to feeling very personally concerned with them and wonder how they get along after I'm gone."

"That's something you'll have to get over, if you go into nursing," Sara cautioned. "You must learn not to take the patients home with you, otherwise you'll get to be a nervous wreck —not much good to yourself or to them."

But how did one get over feeling sorry for people? Bonnie wondered. Even doctors didn't always. Look at the Resident, Dr. Guthrie. When she first came to the Center she used to be terrified of him, until she discovered that his gruff exterior covered a marshmallow heart. She had seen him working with the really sick people and with children—little Wendy Martin, in Pediatrics that time. He had a wonderful gentleness about him, even though his craggy face might be wearing a frown. After she had observed him a few times she began to sense the anger coupled with the gentleness, an anger against disease. Of course he was never sentimental, but she could see how deeply he felt for people. Maybe there were times when he regretted being a doctor.

"Say, Bon, are you with us?" Pixie asked, jogging her friend's elbow. "What are you thinking about, anyhow?"

"Oh-h, nothing important," Bonnie said. "I

guess it's time for us to get back, huh? 'Bye, Sara."

"Slave driver," Pixie grumbled, following her good-humoredly nevertheless. "You'd think we were being paid to sacrifice our young lives like this."

"Well, maybe you'll do such good work you'll get a raise someday," Bonnie suggested.

"Oh, sure," Pixie said. "A raise from nothing to nothing more. However, I am serving humanity, am I not?"

"If you want to call it that," Bonnie taunted.

"I do!" Pixie said. "I'm sure the recovery rate at the center has more than doubled since I've been here."

Bonnie laughed. Pixie was fun. With her you were always assured of seeing the lighter side of things. For the first time since Anne had moved away she felt close to another girl. Perhaps she and Pixie would become real friends.

Suddenly Pixie stopped. "Say, are you going to the picnic-swim next Thursday?"

"I certainly am!"

"It'll be fun to see how the other half lives," Pixie remarked. "The Warren Tilford estate looks out of this world from the little one can see from the road."

"You shameless worshiper of the idle rich!" Bonnie said.

"Oh, no!" Pixie's pony tail swished. "Mr. Tilford is anything but. My father says he built that chemical plant of his from the ground up practically with his bare hands. And now it's one of the most important in the country, with all sorts of government contracts. Mr. Tilford is on the job himself at eight o'clock every morning."

"Goodness, how do you know all this?" Pixie's serious side never failed to amaze Bonnie.

"My Dad is a sales representative for the firm. I thought you knew. Mr. Tilford is a research chemist, with umpteen degrees after his name and all sorts of honors. He has a private research lab next to his office and comes up with terrific formulas every now and then. Why, he even lives near the plant, so he can get back and forth in a matter of minutes."

"He sounds like one of your personal heroes." Bonnie was quite impressed herself.

"He is one of Dad's," Pixie admitted. "A really swell guy. And a very public-spirited citizen. He gave Hamilton most of the Clinic, in memory of his son who was killed in the war. There's a plaque on the wall there someplace. Look it up."

"I will!" Bonnie promised. "And to quote my father, living memorials like that are so much more sensible than those pigeon-roost statues in the parks."

"That's what my father says, too," Pixie gave an affirmative nod.

But Bonnie's attention had wandered away. Now she was more concerned with the coming picnic than with memorials or the people who gave them. David Adams would be at the picnic!

"What time are you coming over?" Pixie asked.

"To the picnic?" Bonnie looked vague.

"No! To my pajama party! Tonight! Where do you go inside that head of yours? Can you make it around eight?"

"Oh! Yes, of course," Bonnie said.

"Don't eat too much supper. Plan to gorge at my house." She clapped herself on the forehead. "What am I doing letting you talk me into going upstairs again? I'm signing out. I have a trillion things to do. G'by. See you later."

"Eight o'clock," Bonnie said, and stepped into the elevator.

fourteen

"I'M GLAD YOU'RE GETTING OUT WITH A NICE group of girls," Mrs. Schuyler said, bringing in a fresh summer-weight blanket from the linen closet for Bonnie. "I know you've missed Anne, but partings of one kind or another come to us all through life and we have to adjust to them. It's good to have lots of friends."

Bonnie nodded. "I think I've made several new ones through the Medical Center. We get to know each other pretty well whenever we meet after duty or on Courier Service, when we have a little time to sit down and talk. I like Pixie Chase best."

She packed her pajamas, a housecoat, and toilet articles in an overnight case and set it on top of her pillow, the summer blanket, and a flower quilt which would serve as a mattress. "We're all going to sleep on the floor in Pixie's living room," she told her mother. "Mr. Chase is away, so we won't be putting him out, and can watch television and play records till all hours. I don't think we'll get much sleep."

"No, I don't imagine you will," Mother laughed. "It reminds me of the dorm parties we used to have when I was in boarding school. They were fun, but we did have a curfew. Are you all together now? If so, I'm ready to drive you over."

Laura met them on the way down the stairs. "Oh, boy!" she shouted. "You moving out, Bon? You mean I can have our room all to myself?"

"Just for tonight," Bonnie reminded her sister with mock severity. "And I'd better not find your things scattered all over the place when I get home tomorrow. You keep everything neat."

"Bonnie 'Neat' Schuyler," Laura teased. "I never saw anyone so keen on having everything in order."

"It's a trait you might cultivate," Mother said, pausing to give her younger daughter a hug.

"Have fun!" Laura told Bonnie. "I'll probably miss you, but don't count on it."

"Brat," Bonnie said fondly, and ran down the last few steps laughing.

Pixie lived in a long, low ranch-type house. The living room was spacious, and even with ten girls crowded in it, there seemed plenty of room. Mrs. Chase greeted each one cordially, and then went upstairs, leaving Pixie in charge.

"You man the phonograph, Bon," Pixie said, "while I check my pizzas in the oven. The last ones are almost ready." She brushed a smudge of flour off her nose and raced to the kitchen.

As Bonnie selected a stack of pop records she glanced over the crowd. Denise and Carol were there, but all the rest were girls she knew only through school.

Ruth Cowan sprawled in an easy chair and declared loudly, "I am going to let Pixie wait on me hand and foot after working at Abbott's all day. I used to go there for sodas and ice cream after school, but you should see it on weekdays at noon when all the hungry office-workers flock in! All those jaws chomping away!"

"Don't complain, at least you were able to get a job," Edith Hurd said. "I wasn't, so I guess my fall wardrobe isn't going to be as lavish as I'd hoped."

"Wardrobe, nothing! I'm saving for college," Ruth said.

Pam Jones chimed in above the pop singer's voice. "I'm lucky. Working in a department store I get an employee's discount, and does that help!"

While the girls were exclaiming over Pam's happy situation, Pixie returned. "I've put all the pies to keep warm for us until midnight. I think we'll be ready for them about then. What's new with everybody? Since I've been at the Medical Center I don't see anybody. Isn't that the way it is with you, too, Bon?"

Bonnie nodded.

"Still, the most interesting things must be happening to you, girls," Ruth said, "considering what you are doing with your summer. I wish I'd thought to become a Candy Striper —especially since I'm still undecided as to whether I want to go into teaching or nursing. Nursing sounds more exciting."

"Well, I suppose it is, in a way, but it's not all fun, being with sick people, you know," Pixie pointed out. "In fact, I've about decided it's not for me, though I might go for being a technician, or a dietician or something like that.

There's lots more to hospital work than just nursing."

"But all the cases you must see," Ruth persisted. "Tell us about them."

"I guess the Clinic is the most interesting for that," Pixie said, "because all sorts of unexpected things happen and the Candy Stripers there can see the actual treatments. You were in the Clinic this afternoon, weren't you, Bonnie? Anything exciting happen?" Pixie drew Bonnie into the group skillfully and turned down the volume on a blaring record.

"You should have Nancy Wheeler here to tell you about the Clinic," Bonnie said. "She practically lives down there and all the nurses and doctors really depend on her. I took care of a little girl today who was waiting to have a fractured arm set. She and her mother were in a car smashup and her mother was admitted upstairs because she was quite badly hurt. The little girl was a bit younger than my sister, Laura," Bonnie said, recalling the scene in the fracture room.

Little Mary Esposito had been so worried about her mother who had been rushed away on a stretcher. "Will Mommy be all right?" she kept asking Bonnie every few minutes.

"Yes," Bonnie told her each time, brushing back the tumbled dark hair. "The doctors are

taking care of her now. She'll be all right."
Little Mary would relax, and then the question
would come again.

But would the mother be "all right?"
Bonnie wondered uneasily, and finally slipped
away to find out through Miss Perkins when
the results of X-rays and preliminary exami-
nations could be known.

Returning to Mary, she was able to report
that her mother would, indeed, be "all right."
And when the time came for the child to be
anesthetized, she went under in a serene frame
of mind.

Dr. Guthrie came down to set the arm, and
after a sharp glance at Bonnie asked her to
hold Mary's fingers in a certain position so
that the small bones would stay in place as he
wound the wet plaster cast bandages around
the arm. It gave Bonnie a very strange feeling to hold the flaccid fingers—and she tried to
express it to the girls listening to her now.

Edith Hurd shivered. "Oooh," she said. "I
couldn't have done it. It must have felt awful."

"No," Bonnie told her. "I got used to it. And
then when she reacted, returned to consciousness, that is, it was as if I'd been important in
patching her up."

Dr. Guthrie had said, "Stay with her until
she is fully conscious," and then added, with a

quick flash of an unexpected smile, "please."

And then Mary's father had rushed in, full of concern after seeing his wife upstairs. Bonnie assured him that the little girl was all right.

"Say, aren't you awfully young to be a student nurse?" Mr. Esposito asked.

"I would be," Bonnie told him, laughing. "I'm a junior volunteer aide." And then she had to explain to him about the Candy Stripers and the Pink Ladies.

"You mean you people take care of sick and hurt folks, for nothing?" The thought seemed absolutely new to him, but he listened to her with respect, and even admiration. When she finished, to her dismay, he pulled out a wallet and extracted a five-dollar bill.

"Here," he said, "go out and buy yourself something."

"And did you?" Pixie's guests asked in a chorus.

"Of course not!" Bonnie was shocked. "We can't accept tips. I told him as nicely as I knew how, and then I said that if he wished, he could put that money in the building fund; so he went right upstairs and did it.

"And right after he left, a wild-eyed young man burst in shouting for someone to bring a stretcher for his wife right away. Miss Perkins was down the hall and I was just petrified, not knowing what in the world was the matter with his wife. I started to get the stretcher, when Miss Perkins came and took over."

"What was the matter with her?" Ruth was no longer sprawling in the easy chair but sitting at attention.

"She was going to have a baby. Miss Perkins hustled her upstairs in a wheel chair, and she said they just barely got to the Delivery Room in time!"

"Whew!" Ruth said. "Something seems to happen to you girls every minute. And my summer's been so dull!"

The other Candy Stripers had to recount their experiences, and the nonhospital girls sat around and listened avidly. "Gosh," one of them breathed, "you kids are really working with Life, aren't you, while the rest of us are still growing up."

Bonnie thought that over curiously. Why did medical details always hold such an interest for people, especially those on the "outside?" Unconsciously she allied herself with those "on the inside" and when she became aware of it, pushed the idea from her. No thank you, she'd have had all the "inside" she wanted after this summer. There was no romance in it for her.

The talk turned to other things now—boys

and summer fun—and boys—school, clothes—and boys.

"You sure must miss Rock Caldwell this summer," Pam said to Bonnie. "You were such a twosome in school."

But she hadn't, Bonnie thought. She hadn't missed Rock at all, except for the first few days after he left. She had been busy—and then David had come into her life.

"Lucky you, with Cliff Coburn living right next door," Edith remarked. "Has he dated you much?"

"Oh, we're just neighbors." Bonnie tossed it off lightly. If they only knew! Cliff didn't know she was alive, and now that she thought of it again, it was rather maddening. It could ruin a girl's ego—and probably would have hers, except for David. With David around, what did she care about Cliff. Nowadays she thought about David so much that it was almost as if she were with him, dating and having fun, instead of having only an occasional ride home in his half-convertible. But on Thursday she would have a chance really to work on David.

Pixie's party was a success. There was gossip and jokes. They danced on the screened tiled porch and they ate and ate and ate.

"I wanted to have Ginny Lou over," Pixie whispered to Bonnie, "but with that diet of hers, I didn't have the heart to expose her to so much temptation."

It was after three before the phonograph was finally stilled, and the weary girls stretched out on their quilts, spread side by side over the living room floor. We look like refugees from something or other, Bonnie decided just before her heavy eyelids closed.

After a breakfast of pancakes and sausages, the girls scattered to their homes. It had been a wonderful party, and Pixie a fine hostess. But it took Bonnie the rest of Saturday and most of Sunday to get over the effects of such a late night.

By Monday morning she had recovered her pep and energy—and the first person she saw at the Medical Center was David. It was almost as if he'd been waiting for her to come through the door, she thought, even though he did pick up some keys at the Information Desk. "See you at lunch," David said, with his nice warm smile, before swinging off toward Pathology—and in the evening he drove her home. But he still did not ask her for a date!

Well, she'd take care of that Thursday! She would wear her prettiest playsuit to the picnic, and take along her most becoming bathing suit, and she would be so charming that . . .

"Going up?" a maintenance man asked from

the open elevator door and spoiled the happy conclusion of her plans.

Thursday was perfect. Hot, sunny. Swimming weather. And yet it felt almost unnatural to Bonnie to be dressing in shorts and a sleeveless blouse instead of her pink-striped uniform.

At the breakfast table Laura buttered toast grumpily. "Lucky you," she said, in what was becoming a refrain. "I wish I were going to this picnic-swim, too. I'll bet they have a scrumptious pool a mile long. I'll bet it's almost as nice as going to the shore."

Bonnie looked at her younger sister in surprise. It had been weeks since she had thought regretfully about the shore. And up to now she had never considered how Laura might have felt about being deprived of it, for however worthy a cause. She reached over and patted her sister's round arm. "I wish you were going, pet. I'd take you if I could."

"I know," Laura said. "It's just that I feel grousey this morning. Is your David going to be there?"

A telltale blush colored Bonnie's face. "He's not 'my' David," she said.

"Oh, yes," Father looked up, "is that the boy who's been bringing you home? Why haven't you asked him in? Or for dinner? I'm sure you and Mother could have arranged it."

"Isn't he a little old for Bonnie?" Mother asked. "I think you said he was in college, didn't you, dear?"

Here we go again, Bonnie thought. "Yes," she answered, looking daggers at Laura—who, as usual, belatedly appeared sorry. "That doesn't make him forty years old."

"Of course not," Mother agreed soothingly. "And if you'd like to invite him, you certainly may. I think I mentioned it before."

"Yes, Mother. Thank you."

"Why not make it this Sunday, then?" Father asked. He seemed in an absolute passion to meet David, Bonnie thought; and she certainly did not feel like explaining that she'd prefer to have David ask her out for a real date first.

"All right," she said. "I will." If she didn't agree, her parents might think there was something wrong with David.

"Oh, boy; and I promise I won't say a thing I shouldn't!" Laura said.

Suddenly Bonnie laughed. "That will be the day."

"Who's picking you up?" the irrepressible Laura was off again.

"Rickie Page and Nancy—and David," Bonnie told her. "At eleven."

"Oh, I'm sorry. I won't be home then," Mother said. "I have a dental appointment."

But it wasn't David's ancient half-convertible that pulled up in front of the Schuyler house at eleven. Instead, a long gleaming black and silver Continental purred into the drive, with Rickie Page at the wheel.

"I must apologize for this magnificence," David said, getting out. "But alas, my chariot developed internal noncombustion with complications and had to be hauled off ignominiously to a garage. You and Nancy will just have to be content with all—this." He made it sound like such a catastrophe that Bonnie burst out laughing.

Rickie jumped out on the other side, grinning. "Courtesy of my father," he explained. "It will be eons before I can even afford to think in terms like these." He sprinted across the lawn to Nancy's house.

Left alone with her, David looked Bonnie up and down and seemed to like what he saw. "I almost don't know you without your uniform," he said.

"But it's me all right. Honest!" Bonnie assured him.

"Oh, I'm satisfied," he said, and added, "we're supposed to pick up some more people. Pixie Chase, Denise. . . . Mrs. Brent gave us a list, and you and Nancy can tell us how to find the different streets." He glanced toward the house and saw Laura on the porch.

Bonnie introduced them quickly and explained about her mother. "But both Mother and Father would like to meet you," she added. "Can you have dinner with us Sunday?"

"I most certainly can," David said. He seemed so genuinely pleased by the invitation that Bonnie forgot about her qualms. What if he hadn't dated her! He had been bringing her home, and now she was assured of another whole afternoon with him!

Ricky rejoined them with Nancy, and the quartet drove off to pick up the others. With the car full, they pulled into the Tilford carport, which was about the size of a parking lot.

A tall boy detached himself from the seat of a large power mower and came over to direct them to the swimming pool, hidden behind an evergreen hedge.

The voice was familiar, and Bonnie, who had been laughing up at David, glanced at the boy. It was Cliff Coburn! Was he working on the estate? If Cliff recognized her, he gave no sign of it. His eyes were cool as he inspected the luxurious car and the carefree group clambering out of it. Somehow Bonnie got the feeling that he was critical of all of them. She would have spoken to him, but she was too annoyed, and so she passed by him.

At sight of the pool she forgot all about Cliff. It was huge, and painted a clear, luxurious blue-green that had an almost magnetic pull. The terrace around it was dotted with tables, shaded by colorful umbrellas, like mushrooms in fairyland, and across a strip of lawn were the dressing rooms, in a long tile-roofed cabana. A uniformed maid and a houseman, in a white jacket, hovered nearby. Laughing young people, earlier arrivals, were popping out of the dressing room doors and dashing into the pool with giggles and joyous shrieks.

"I see no sign of our hostess, so I guess that's what we're supposed to do, too," Bonnie surmised, glancing at the maid.

"Yes, miss, you sure are," the woman responded with a broad, friendly smile. "The ladies come this way," she added.

"And the gentlemen, around the other side," the houseman said.

"See you later, fellows!" Pixie caroled. "Isn't this the life!"

At noon, Mrs. Warren Tilford appeared simultaneously with a tray parade of picnic food. She was a small, gray-haired lady,

dressed in a simple linen frock, her face serene
and a cordial smile on her lips. The young people liked her at once as she made them welcome and supervised the setting up of trays.
Portable grills were wheeled in, and several
boys appointed themselves chefs, appropriating
the starched white hats the houseman supplied
as badges of their office. Cliff Coburn, Bonnie
noticed, made himself unobtrusively useful,
bringing in additional equipment, starting
charcoal fires and setting up more chairs. He
was very efficient, and Mrs. Tilford thanked
him before leaving the young people to their
own devices.

This holiday had a heavenly quality to it
Bonnie thought, as she lolled on a chaise
longue after lunch. David lay stretched full
length on the grass near her and she watched
him through half-closed eyes, admiring his
broad shoulders, his well-shaped head with the
close-set ears, the heavy eyebrows, so much
darker than his fair hair.

A cloud went over the sun and a breath of
coolness swept over the lawn. Bonnie shivered.
Summer was waning. School would begin soon,
and that meant that school would begin for
David, too. He would be going away. Still, Co-
lumbia University wasn't so distant. Lots of people in Hamilton commuted to New York City

daily. David could come and visit week ends, and perhaps she could go to some of the football games at Baker Field, and whatever dances they happened to have. Maybe he'd give her his heavy gold ring to put on a chain around her neck, for all to see. It would be thrilling to go with a college man.

She would have to tell Rock Caldwell about David, of course. Rock had phoned her from the camp last week end and badgered her about not writing him more often. For just a second she saw Rock in David's place on the grass, bronzed by his summer in the sun, and heavier built, more muscular, with his very blond hair even blonder, and the cute cleft in his rather square chin. She glanced away from the prone figure, straight into Cliff Coburn's eyes and a blush leaped into her cheeks. Cliff turned away at once, but how long had he been staring at her?

She sat up and swung her legs off the chaise. "Come on, David, I'll race you to the other end of the pool!"

"Huh?" He opened one eye lazily, and she grabbed a hand and tugged him to his feet. The next moment they were flying across the grass, hand in hand, leaping into the depths of the cool water that closed over their heads with a swirl and roar in the ears. Bobbing to the surface, they swam side by side, with strong, even strokes, the length of the pool.

They touched the rim, turned, and pushed off again with one accord, with perfect understanding, Bonnie thought. Suddenly David dived under water and grabbed her heels, pulling her down, down, squealing and kicking. When she came up again, sputtering, his face was close to hers. She gasped for breath, and treading water, he held her up. It was thrilling to rest in the circle of his arm. She looked at him trying to keep her heart out of her eyes. He was like a laughing young merman, with drops of water beading his short, thick eyelashes.

Oh, David, I love you! she cried silently, eloquently, behind her own closed lids.

He leaned forward and kissed the tip of her nose. Bonnie went faint with delight.

Friday morning was gray with fog, chilly and damp with a steady drizzle of rain. Bonnie and Nancy, waiting for the bus, shivered under their dripping raincoats and hats.

Later, on Courier Duty, Bonnie thought that if it weren't for the tender sunburned areas under her shoulder straps, she would never have believed that yesterday's picnic-swim had actually happened. Most of the other Candy Stripers went around easing their straps just as often as she did, except Ginny Lou.

"Why on earth didn't you go?" Bonnie asked when she returned from an errand and they were temporarily alone. "It was really divine."

"I know," Ginny Lou sighed. "But if you'd ever seen me in a bathing suit, you wouldn't ask. I've lost ten pounds so far. Ten more and I'm going to look human. Why, even Dr. Guthrie is pleased with me. He *smiled* at me the last time he weighed me!"

"That is an achievement!" Bonnie laughed. "He's usually so preoccupied fighting the demons of pain and disease."

"Well," Ginny Lou confessed, "maybe Miss Kent's being down in the Clinic at the time helped a little. I think she's broken down his resistance. I even saw them in town together the other day. Near a jeweler!"

"You did? We'll have to capture Carol and pump her."

"Let's!" Ginny Lou was all for the idea. "I'm sure I scent romance. I can't believe they were just taking a walk in front of Lyon's Jewelry. We'll grab Carol at lunch and find out what she knows."

But when lunchtime rolled around, no one at the Medical Center was in the Cafeteria, and pumping Carol was furthest from Bonnie's thoughts.

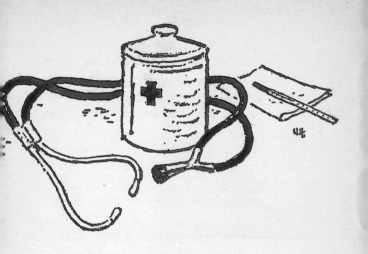

fifteen

AT ELEVEN-TEN NANCY WAS FILLING OUT A new chart for an auto accident victim being treated for head cuts. "We're going to have a lot more of these if that fog keeps up," she remarked, glancing out of the window.

"I'm afraid you're right," Miss Perkins, coming in with a patient's specimen in a tube, agreed reluctantly. "We'll hope for the best anyway. Bonnie, will you take this up to the lab?"

Bonnie reached for the test tube. Her fingers curled around it.

Then it happened.

A tremendous BOOM seemed to rock the building. Windows rattled, and the wide emergency doors swung inward on their hinges from the concussion. A series of duller explosions ripped the air, followed by a moment of unearthly shocked silence, and then sirens began to shriek all over town.

Nancy had jumped to her feet, but Bonnie stood frozen where she was, the test tube shattered at her feet.

"The powder plant," Miss Perkins gasped. "Or the arsenal. I heard it go just like that ten years ago. O my Lord, girls, we're really going to see something now." She closed her eyes in a hasty prayer.

The telephone began to jangle; nurses, aides, students and interns streamed down to the Clinic from all parts of the building. The waiting room was cleared of all non-emergency cases, and, while nurses set up emergency treatment equipment, corpsmen and orderlies assembled stretchers from every floor and storeroom. Candy Stripers, pale or flushed with excitement, were sent on a million errands. They covered stretchers, treatment and examining tables, assembled piles of sheets and blankets, brought down IV poles for immediate infusions of whole blood or plasma. The orderly quiet of the Center seemed to have vanished in the instant of that first terrible blast.

"Get a paper towel and clean up that test tube mess," Miss Perkins ordered between telephone calls. "Never mind about that specimen now."

Bonnie obeyed mechanically, the explosion still roaring in her ears, and then scurried to help the nurses and orderlies. Everyone on the hospital staff seemed to be expecting an inundation of the injuried. How badly would they be hurt? She could hear the anxious hammering of her heart and her stomach muscles tightened. As the wails of the first ambulances began to draw nearer and nearer, Bonnie prayed fervently that she would not get sick or faint.

Nurses off duty began hurrying in; doctors' cars careened into the parking area, as all available physicians arrived for the emergency.

Ambulances backed up to the door, one after the other, and disaster crews from all the nearby towns brought in stretcher after stretcher of victims—men and women, torn and bleeding, some with clothes in tatters, without shoes; others with terrible burns—weeping, moaning— or terribly still!

The Receiving and Accident Rooms were filled in no time, doctors and nurses proceeding at once with treatment of the worst injured, sending others directly to the major operating rooms upstairs. Bonnie clasped her hands tight, staring at the dreadful scene, unable to believe that it was actually happening. She reached out to steady herself against the wall.

"If you're going to be sick, go home!" a severe voice rasped into her ear. "We can't be bothered nursing Candy Stripers on top of the injured."

The words had the effect of a stinging slap, and Bonnie's head jerked around to find Miss Winters frowning at her. Before she could say a word, the nurse was gone, but her challenge had stiffened Bonnie's sagging courage. She'd show Miss Winters that she didn't need to be nursed!

She grabbed a wheel chair and hurried to the door to receive a victim. Blood was trickling down his face, and his arm had a peculiar, unnatural bulge. She did not allow herself to think of that as a nurse told her to take him down the corridor into the waiting room, where the less critically injured were being put for the present.

Nancy helped her wheel a stretcher case into the Fracture Room. Soon every available inch of space appeared filled with victims, and yet more kept coming. In between ambulances the girls tried to comfort the victims as best they could. Sometimes a friendly pat was enough to evoke a tremulous smile, sometimes a few words silenced a moan. Bonnie noticed that although Nancy was pale, she managed to wear an unharried air and even a smile when she talked to individuals able to understand her. Bonnie steeled herself and tried to do the same, but it wasn't easy.

"My eyes! My eyes!" A man, lying on a cot moaned, clutching a bandage that swathed most of his head. "How long before they get to me? How long? Nurse! Nurse!"

About to pass by, Bonnie paused to soothe this victim. "Not too long," she said gently, putting his arms down. "Please lie quietly."

He grabbed and held her hand. *"The Lord is my shepherd . . . The Lord is my shepherd . . ."* he muttered, unable to get past the first few words of the Twenty-Third Psalm.

"I shall not want," Bonnie continued for him, and the man's lips formed the comforting words after her. He relaxed, and with a pitying headshake, she moved on, her eyes stinging with unshed tears.

Station wagons and private cars kept coming, each with its mercy load of victims. Bonnie hurried to the door with a wheel chair to assist a tall boy and a slight woman who were bringing in a big man, leaning heavily upon them. There were burns on the man's face, and one arm was tied up incongruously in a sling made from a pink lacy slip. The boy's hands and face were blackened, his shirt and one pants' leg were torn and he was limping slightly. Under the grime she recognized Cliff Coburn!

He stared at her uncomprehendingly, as if this were the last place in the world where he expected to find her. Didn't he know that she worked at the hospital? Bonnie wondered as she helped get the man into the chair.

The woman hovering over him was Mrs. Tilford! So this must be her husband! Then the explosion had not been at the powder plant or at the arsenal. It must have been at the Warren Tilford Chemical Works. Bonnie tucked a blanket around Mr. Tilford and at a nurse's nod, started to wheel him away.

Cliff fell in step with her. "I didn't know you worked here," he said. "Ye gods, what a mess. All these people. Do you suppose I could help?"

"I'm sure you could," Bonnie told him. "There are so many. Just talking to some of them or holding their hands helps. What on earth happened?"

He shook his head and raked his fingers through his hair. "It's hard to believe, but a small passenger plane caused all this. Pilot got lost in the fog, I guess, hit the smokestack at

the Tilford Works and crashed into a section
where they were processing highly explosive
stuff. The thing set off a chain reaction that
must have been heard for miles—but nobody
will ever know the straight of it because the
plane and whoever was in it were blown to
pieces. He bit his lips and shuddered.

"Did you see it? How did you get into this?"
Bonnie asked, but Cliff had dropped back to
talk to a man who had taken hold of his leg
as they went by his low stretcher.

Bonnie left the Tilfords and hurried back
toward the entrance. A nurse stopped her.
"Wash these instruments. Utility room," she
said, thrusting a tray into her hands.

Sara Foster, the student nurse, was busily
packing cleaned instruments and rubber gloves
into sterilizing cases, slipping them into the
steaming autoclave. Bonnie set to work, scrub-
bing swiftly but carefully in a basin filled with
antiseptic solution. Sara was pale, but her
hands moved rhythmically, the fingers deft.

"What do you think of nursing now?" she
asked, a rueful smile flitting across her tired
face.

The question took Bonnie by surprise. "I—
don't know," she said. "It's terribly necessary,
isn't it?"

"Today it certainly is," Sara agreed. "But I

had to escort a couple of Candy Stripers out. They couldn't stand the sight of so much blood. It doesn't seem to bother you."

"No," Bonnie admitted. "Not much—at least, not after the first shock wore off. I felt all gone, and then I wouldn't let myself think about it."

Sara nodded. "You have to sort of accept it. When I first went into training I wondered how I'd react to blood. A lot of it, I mean. The first time I saw it gushing from a wound I did feel faint, but then I concentrated on its color. Blood is such a bright, living red—and we were helping the patient, so it wasn't as if his life were flowing away. It got me over the bad spot, and I've used that thought ever since. Do you know, there are some surgeons who have to steel themselves against the sight of blood? One of them told me he used to pass out regularly as a student, and he wasn't the only one."

And yet he went on and became a surgeon! Bonnie mulled that over.

The stream of instruments to clean was unending, but finally someone came to relieve her, and Bonnie went back into the corridors. There were no more new arrivals, but still many injured waiting for care.

"Hold this!" a harsh voice said, thrusting a jar of plasma into her hands. "There just isn't another IV pole available. Steady—and this high."

Bonnie stared at the patient, an elderly man. His arm was strapped down and a needle was inserted into a vein in the forearm. His eyes flickered momentarily. She glanced at the nurse. Miss Winters!

"He's in shock," she said. "Hold it steady now."

Bonnie held the plasma jar as if her own life depended on it.

"I see you're still here," Miss Winters commented, eying her up and down. "And you look as if you've been busy."

Bonnie glanced at her uniform and was horrified by its appearance—rumpled, stained, one pocket half torn. "I guess I have," she said, keeping the jar steady.

"Good girl." Unexpectedly Miss Winters smiled. Her eyes were kind. "I'm afraid I've misjudged you," and she was gone to tend to another patient.

Coming from Miss Winters this was an accolade. Bonnie gaped after the elderly nurse and some of the weariness seemed to leave her body. When Miss Winters said a kind word like that, it really meant something!

But, as she continued to hold the inverted plasma jar, it grew heavier and heavier, the drops of precious fluid flowing with excruciating slowness down the plastic tube into the vein of the injured man. Bonnie's head began to throb, and her arms ached intolerably. The empty sensation in her stomach reminded her that along with everybody else down here she had not had lunch. Breakfast seemed years away. In fact, everything that had ever happened to her prior to this moment seemed years away. Even yesterday and the picnic-swim and David. She had had just one glimpse of him today, on an errand to the lab. He was working on emergency tests, each of which had to be done *"stat!"* At once, or sooner!

Just as Bonnie began to think that she could not hold the plasma jar another moment, someone took it from her and hung it on an IV pole which materialized as if by magic. She blinked gratefully, her arms dropping to her sides.

"You look bushed," Cliff said. "That nurse, what's-her-name, Miss Winters, told me to bring this thing over and hang your jar on it."

"I shall never look at an IV pole again without loving every inch of it," Bonnie declared. "And golly, I am bushed."

"Well, things are quieting down. Everything's under control and fresh people are coming in to relieve the regular staff. Miss Winters said to take you up to the cafeteria and see that you have something to eat—you and any other Candy Stripers still around. What is she, your Guardian Angel?"

Bonnie stared at him. If Cliff could only know how funny that remark was. And yet, today, Miss Winters had looked at her almost with downright affection. Perhaps, in her own peculiar, severe way, Miss Winters was her guardian angel, and the guardian angel of every other young girl learning her way around the hospital. Anyone coming into the sphere of her discipline certainly would not take hospital work lightly. It was serious business, and Miss Winters never failed to point that out. Why, Bonnie thought, she was getting almost fond of the starched White Dragon!

She followed as Cliff led the way, but not without a backward look at the people still in the corridors. Nurses and aides in fresh uniforms were among them now, doing what was necessary. She sighed as they waited for the elevator to come down. The cafeteria was only a flight up, but Bonnie felt she couldn't raise one foot above the other to make the stairs.

"Do you work in the emergency clinic often?" Cliff asked. His eyes seemed to hold a new respect for her.

"Fairly often," she said. "But this," she waved

back in the direction of the Clinic, "never happened to me before."

"I should hope not," he said fervently. "Just helping out the way I did, I got a real dose of this sort of thing."

"How did you get into it?" Bonnie asked. "On the scene, I mean."

"I was working in the garage at the Tilford's, polishing their station wagon when it happened. The garage windows shattered, and half of those in the house, too. I thought we were being bombed. But Mrs. Tilford seemed to know it was the plant right away and came tearing out of the house, her face wild. She jumped into the station wagon without even seeing me. She wasn't in any shape to drive, so before she could start the motor, I lunged in, pushed her over and took her to the plant. There was no reasoning with her. She kept moaning, 'Warren's in there! Warren's in there!' Over and over."

"Poor thing," Bonnie murmured sympathetically.

"Down there it was awful," Cliff continued. "We were among the first to arrive. The place was a shambles, steaming and smoking, with flames beginning to lick out of the ruins. Like a scene of a bombing in a movie, only this was for real, with the injured screaming and running and crawling out of the building, or being dragged out by their fellows. The smell of the burning and exploding chemicals was nauseating. People were coughing and choking on top of everything else.

"I don't know how Mrs. Tilford found her husband, but she did, and she tore off her slip and made that sling for his arm. Then the two of us dragged him away from the plant. He had been right in there, trying to help the other injured, although his own arm was broken and there was an awful lump on his head, not to mention his chemical burns. We gathered up as many as we could in the station wagon and boiled down here.

"You were swell, Bonnie. I hadn't—I mean, I didn't—well, you know. Every time I saw you, you were with a different guy, or out having a whale of a good time, like at the picnic. Golly, was that only yesterday? I thought—" His face, which he had somehow found time to wash, turned brick red.

Bonnie was about to ease his embarrassment when they were swept into the elevator. Her halo was getting almost too big to wear, she thought, amused.

The cafeteria was filled with tired, grubby people, clutching cups of coffee and gulping sandwiches and doughnuts. There was Rocheen

Kent, leaning her weary head on one hand, and
Dr. Tom Guthrie, hurrying to her with a tray
of food, was looking absolutely ferocious.

"Who's that?" Cliff asked. "He sure looks
fierce."

"He's not really," Bonnie replied. She had
seen Dr. Guthrie handling the injured downstairs. A mother's hands could not have been
more gentle or more sure. "But he gets angry
at sickness and injuries and weariness, too, I
guess, and even at himself," she added with
newborn insight, "because in spite of trying to
take an impersonal attitude, he *feels* for people."

"He sure must feel plenty for that pretty
nurse," Cliff said, grinning.

Bonnie laughed. "So I've heard." Wasn't it
only this morning that she and Ginny Lou had
laid plans to pump Carol about her cousin?
Then she saw David, and in the same instant he
saw her. He rose and came over, and Cliff
seemed to melt away into the crowd.

"I'm going to take you home," David said,
"just as soon as you have something to eat. You
look like you've had it."

"So do you," she countered.

"No matter how rushed we were in the lab, it
was nothing to what a youngster like you had to
face downstairs."

She flinched at the word "youngster," but

David's concern over her wiped it out of her mind.

What had happened to Cliff? she wondered in weary lassitude later as she and David rattled away in his repaired half-convertible. The drizzle had stopped, so it did not matter that the old canvas top would not go up. The interior had been protected by a tarpaulin, but she would have gladly ridden with him through a downpour, up to her neck in water, especially now, with only a few days left of her regular work at the Medical Center, of being able to have at least a glimpse of him every day.

She was sure that David cared for her. Perhaps not quite the way she cared for him, but she'd have to find out before they returned to their separate schools. He was coming for dinner on Sunday. She was so glad now that her family had practically made her ask him—and then he would probably ask her out on a date, or maybe for a drive that very afternoon.

Bonnie closed her eyes. She could almost fool David's arms around her, his lips on hers, as he told her that he loved her, too. . . .

sixteen

SHE WAS SO PROUD OF DAVID ON SUNDAY. HE AR-
rived precisely on time, his casual slacks and
sports jacket neatly pressed, his fair hair slicked
down, but with that stubborn wave showing,
nevertheless. His glance rested approvingly on
her smooth pageboy, burnished until it shone;
on the cornflower blue dress that accentuated
her eyes. His hand was warm on hers. He
greeted her mother with just the right degree
of deference, and Bonnie noted how firm his
grip was when he took her father's hand, and
how sweet he was to Laura. She wondered suddenly if he had a sister.

"He's nice," Laura whispered as the girls were setting the table. "Dad likes him, too. Aren't you the lucky one with all these fellows on your doorstep!"

"All what fellows?" Bonnie asked.

"Why, Rock, and David, and Cliff Coburn. As if you didn't know!"

"Cliff?" Bonnie's eyebrows arched and the silver she was holding clattered in her hand.

"Sure. I talked to him yesterday, and he said he thought you were just wonderful at the Center the other day."

"Oh?" Bonnie smiled, but rather absently. David had suggested a drive after dinner. That was more important than what Cliff thought of her. Things were working out beautifully.

She scarcely knew what she ate during dinner, or what precisely was being said, for thinking of going off with David afterward. The small talk drifted around her, with only David's voice coming through as he spoke of his own home in Chicago and his family and his future plans. She sensed that her parents liked him—but who could help liking David?

They were to have dessert on the patio, and while she helped serve it, Mother said, "He is a charming young man and he seemes to miss his home and family a great deal. We should have had him out here before."

"I know," Bonnie said, regretfully. David fitted into the family group so perfectly.

Shortly after dessert they left for their drive.

The countryside streamed past them: sunlit fields, stretches of woods, farmlands, and then a gradual rise into the hills. They were heading for Echo Lake. An Indian maiden was supposed to have cast herself into it from a cliff because of a faithless lover, and it was claimed that her brokenhearted cry as she plunged into the water was still heard over the lake. Bonnie shivered and moved closer to David.

He pulled up almost to the water's edge and they sat in the car, watching birds skimming the surface, their wing tips sometimes ruffling the water, their cries repeated by echoes from the cliff.

"I'm going to hate leaving all this and going back to my city campus," David said, sighing. "I like your Hamilton, Bonnie; the country around it. And the people." He leaned over and tipped her chin up. "You're a sweet girl, and very pretty."

"Oh, David!" She clasped his hand in both of hers, her heart in her eyes. "I'm going to miss you, too."

"You are? With all the Hamilton fellows beating a path to your door?"

"I don't care about them!"

"Not even that neighbor of yours who kept peering at us from behind the hedge every moment we were outside at your house?"

"Don't tease, David. I—I've never felt like this about anyone before."

He stared at her, startled.

"Oh, David," she whispered. "I'm so in love with you," and buried her head in his shoulder.

She did not see the alarm in his eyes. For a moment he sat rigid, then his arms went around her gently. One hand stroked her hair. He seemed to be groping for words.

"Bonnie," he said softly, "you're still such a baby. I wouldn't hurt you for the world. I had no idea——"

What was he saying? That didn't sound right! This wasn't the way she had imagined it.

"You're a fine girl, Bonnie. Sweet and lovely as a breath of spring. But, I've thought of you —well, the way I'd think of my own young sister. You even look a bit like Kathy——"

"*Oh!*" She pushed away from him, horrified. He had mentioned a sister at the table! Was that all she'd been to him then? A reminder of his *sister!* There was no mistaking the sincerity —or the finality—of his words. With a stifled moan she flung herself away from him and hid her head in her arms. What had she done, speaking out like that! How could she ever face him again? A hot tide of shame washed over her. She had taken so much for granted. Misinterpreted, misunderstood so much, not because of the way David had acted, she saw with painful clarity, but because she had wanted it that way. The whole romance had been only in her mind. *Oh, David, David!* She wept brokenly.

He reached over and gave her a panicky pat on the back. "Don't cry, Bonnie. Please. You'll —you'll forget all about this. Honest you will. When you go back to school, among your old friends you won't even think about this. Why, Bonnie, I'm twenty-two. Much too old for you now."

He didn't understand. What did a few years one way or the other matter? He didn't understand how dreadfully empty and forsaken she felt because he did not love her. If she could just get away from him, so he would not see how humiliated she was.

David took hold of her firmly and turned her around toward him. "Star Girl," he said, "believe me, I am truly sorry. If in any way this is my fault, if I can do anything——"

Just love me, Bonnie cried silently, the tears streaming down her face. But you could not plead for love, or command it. It had to be freely given, by one person to another because of some mysterious chemical attraction that drew people together.

Bonnie bent her head, trying to collect herself. David did look miserable. He wasn't being callous about this. He didn't despise her. He was really being kind—*l-like a brother!*

"I'm sorry, David. I'm sorry I imagined things that weren't there," Bonnie told him in a small wooden voice.

"I'd better take you home," he said quietly. But he drove slowly, and along back ways, allowing her to compose herself, to erase the traces of tears.

A soft dusk had fallen by the time they pulled up before her house. Bonnie was still numb with hurt.

"Please thank your parents for having me over today," David said. "I—I don't think I'd better go back in. You'll be all right, won't you?"

She nodded dully.

He got out, came around to her side of the car and opened the door. She stepped unsteadily to the pavement, holding her shoulders stiff, her fingers curled into tight fists.

"Bonnie," he said, catching her arm and making her face him. "I do think you're a wonderful, lovely girl, with lots of happiness ahead."

He took her face between his hands and kissed her tenderly on the forehead.

"Good-by, David," she said. *Good-by, my love.*

Mercifully her parents had gone to play bridge with the Wheelers, a note on the hall table informed her. And Laura was spending the night with a friend. Good, Bonnie thought, for this was one time she didn't want to face her family. She went to bed at once, shattered by her experience. She wondered how she'd find strength and courage and dignity to go to the Medical Center tomorrow, as usual. How could she possibly meet David—as if nothing had happened. It never occurred to her that she could resign.

In the morning, her mother was too full of her own plans to notice how subdued her daughter was.

"Bonnie," she said, "Pat Wheeler talked to me last night about becoming a Pink Lady at the Center. After hearing so much about your work there, I had considered it, but she convinced me. With you girls going back to school, they really need adult help to take your places. I'm going in this week to sign up for the training course!"

"Good." Bonnie tried to work up a suitable enthusiasm for this complete about-face in her mother, but all she could think about was how in the world she'd get through this day at the Center. It seemed to her everyone would know that something awful had happened to her.

But when she stepped into Mrs. Brent's office to sign in, she found the other Candy Stripers buzzing with excitement.

"Isn't it thrilling?" Pixie demanded, catching hold of Bonnie. "I'm so glad it's going to happen while we're still here! Aren't you?"

"What?" Bonnie asked, puzzled. "I don't know what you're talking about."

"The wedding!" Several girls shrilled. "The whole hospital is talking about it!"

"Whose wedding?" Bonnie asked mechanically. She couldn't be less interested in someone else's wedding at this moment.

"Miss Kent's and Dr. Guthrie's!" The chorus was almost deafening.

"Oh!" In spite of her own sorrow, Bonnie's interest kindled. "When?"

"Wednesday! Dr. Tom has received an appointment at the Maynard Clinic and has to leave practically right away, and he and Miss Kent aro going to be married in the Chapel, here! Isn't that super?" Answers flew from all sides.

"We're all invited to be present!" Ginny Lou announced. "Won't Miss Kent make a lovely bride? Carol's going to be Maid of Honor."

Bonnie began to feel as though her face would crack from smiling and her head snap off from nodding agreement to everything. She left for her Fourth Floor duty as soon as she could extricate herself from the group. Rocheen Kent looked radiant. A goddess in love. Even Miss Winters beamed at her, and all the patients seemed to know. Even the very sick ones managed a smile. There was an air of excitement on the whole floor.

I would be radiant like that if David loved me, Bonnie thought, and hurried into the utility room to hide the tears which sprang to her eyes.

The tiny Chapel was festooned with flowers. The immediate family of the couple were in the pews inside, their hospital associates overflowed into the corridor. The Candy Stripers were pressed into the foreground by kindly older people.

"Dearly beloved, we are gathered together . . ."

Bonnie stood there, white-faced. She was Rocheen, in a cloud of white veiling. Dr. Tom was her David. No, not *her* David. She knew that he was in the background somewhere and her heart ached. Suppose she should break down when she saw him! *Concentrate on the cere-*

mony, she told herself. And then the ceremony was over.

The bride and groom were coming out. Confetti and a discreet amount of rice were flying. The wedding cake towered on a specially set table in the Meeting Room upstairs, decorated for the reception by the staff. . . . And then Rocheen slipped away into the Nurses' Residence to change and make her getaway with her Dr. Tom.

Bonnie's lips were stiff from smiling, smiling, smiling.

At last it was all over, and the hospital could settle back into routine.

"Oh, there you are!" Nancy hurried over. "Don't you feel well? Too much excitement?"

"I—have a headache," Bonnie said. "It'll go away."

"Wasn't the wedding perfect?" Nancy asked. "I think it made every one of us girls want to be a bride. But that isn't why I stopped you. I wondered if you'd like to come to the capping ceremony for the girls who have been here two years? We have just so many tickets to give away so I'll save one for you, if you're free on Saturday night."

Nancy's eyes were sparkling with pride and excitement. The little cap she would receive meant a lot to her. But it meant almost nothing to Bonnie at that moment. Still, for Nancy's sake, she worked up an enthusiastic answer.

"Just think!" Nancy burbled. "Next summer I can be a paid assistant here, and every summer after that, and save the money for my school tuition. I hope your headache will get better soon," she added. "Ask the nurse on your floor to give you an aspirin. It might help. Now I must fly!" She whisked into the elevator, leaving Bonnie to go down the one flight to Fourth and Pediatrics.

Thank goodness all this would be over for her soon, Bonnie thought. There were too many places in the hospital that reminded her of David. And wasn't it hysterical, when she was so disenchanted, that her own Mother should be waiting eagerly to come in and do her bit at the Center?

Bonnie entered Pediatrics in a bitter mood, but it wasn't long before the problems of the little patients took her out of herself completely.

"Hello, Bonnie!" a small voice greeted her slowly from a high-sided bed. "Is it dinnertime? Will you feed me?"

It was Sally, back again at the Center, and she remembered that odd mealtime! For some reason this touched Bonnie so deeply that she stepped over and gave the little girl a hug. "Yes, it's almost dinnertime, darling. And I will feed you," she promised.

"I missed you at lunch," Sally told her solemnly. "I like you!" And the fastidious Bonnie somehow did not mind the soupy kiss on her cheek or the thin arms around her neck that disarranged the neat roll of her hair. It wouldn't be for long, she told herself, as she stepped away and hardened her heart.

Only a few more days and she would be free of all the emotion connected with the hospital.

seventeen

THE CAPPING OF THE SENIOR CANDY STRIPERS TOOK place in the Meeting Room. Proud mothers and fathers occupied the front rows. The group of junior Candy Stripers, friends of the girls to be honored, sat in the back.

"I'm going to get me a cap like that someday," Ginny Lou whispered to Bonnie. "I'm going to work here even after school opens. The experience will help me get admitted into the nursing school I've picked out."

Bonnie smiled perfunctorily. No caps for her. She had almost done what she had signed up to do, and then she would forget it.

A piano began to play and the Seniors marched in, two by two, to take their places solemnly at the right of the platform. *The Star Spangled Banner* was sung, and the program was under way. The hospital administrator delivered a greeting, and Mrs. Brent, her eyes bright, outlined briefly the work of the Candy Stripers—the devotion of the girls to duty; the outstanding things they had done, even though they were not trained nurses.

"As in the recent disaster," Mrs. Brent said, "where the Candy Stripers, many of whom are only fourteen and fifteen years old, worked side by side, unflinchingly and tirelessly with the regular staff to help care for the injured.

"In another instance," Mrs. Brent went on, "I know of two Candy Stripers who came in here just this summer, standing by a badly injured baby, patting and comforting her during the most critical hours—administering the Tender Loving Care that was so necessary at the time, while nurses and doctors gave her their medical skill. . . ."

Startled, Bonnie realized that Mrs. Brent was talking about her and Ginny Lou and color leaped into her face!

"These girls, for all their youth, can rise to any occasion," Mrs. Brent continued. "Many of them clearly show the qualifications necessary for nurses: reliability, responsibility, tolerance, generosity, adaptability, an outgoing friendliness, a liking for people; and so precious in many instances, a sense of humor, which acts like an air cushion in easing the jolts of life.

"The need for nurses is greater than ever today and opportunities in the profession are almost unlimited. Today we have 300,000 active registered nurses. We need 50,000 more! That is why it is our hope that among these precious girls there will be many who will feel the call of Service, who will continue from here on into nursing schools and colleges and emerge to carry on in the profession with honor. . . ."

Bonnie's attention began to wander. The future seemed terribly far away, and awfully blank for her. She shifted restlessly, wishing the whole thing over. The sound of Mrs. Brent's voice drifted around her.

She jumped when all the lights were suddenly turned off, leaving only a soft glow over the platform, with its table covered by perky pink-striped and white-banded caps.

Mrs. Collins stepped forward now and lit the single tall candle on another table. From it radiated a circle of smaller, unlit candles.

As Mrs. Brent called each Senior girl's name, she came forward, knelt on a cushion and was capped, and presented with a small candle, ceremoniously lit from the single big one, before she rose and walked back to her place among the others.

Bonnie found herself sitting forward. The circle of light in which the Seniors knelt was like a benediction. The faces of the capped girls, in the glow of their candles, were almost ethereal. There was joy and dedication in them—an almost holy purity—and among the grownups there were sniffs, and hasty dabs at eyes with handkerchiefs.

Automatically Bonnie's hand went to her chest, and although she was out of uniform, she could almost feel the three stars she had earned for her bib. The first time Dad had seen them, all in a row, he'd said, "Looks like you're starting a flag, young lady. Keep it up." He was awfully proud of her hospital work.

The capped girls began to sing—a familiar hymn of dedication, to which words appropriate to this occasion had been set. As Bonnie stood up, she found a mist of tears in her own eyes, and a quick soaring of pride, for she was a part of this ceremony, too, even though she had received no cap—and never would. And suddenly that thought filled her with a vast sadness, because, somehow, with the capping of the Seniors, her own life as a Candy Striper seemed over.

Hospital experiences of the summer came flooding back to her. The first days of her training ... how strange and frightening the Medical Center had been then. The silly mistakes she and all the others had made. That awful business of the cranked up bed they couldn't get down again, and the awesome Miss Winters who wasn't as frosty and flinthearted as she appeared!

She remembered the burned baby she had comforted—home and nicely healed now; the little boy with the eye operation; and frightened Bruce, about to have an appendectomy, whom she had cheered. The girl who met her young husband feeling beautiful despite her broken arms because Bonnie had made her up and given her a permanent; and there was little Sally, in-again-out-again-in-again in a seemingly endless chain of operations. Sally whose mind was a bit slow, but who remembered her and said, "I like you," and gave her the fervent, sloppy little kiss. Bonnie thought she still felt its wetness on her cheek, but when she raised her hand she found tears under her fingers.

Why was she crying? Because she was about to leave all the pain and heartache of a hospital, or because she was turning her back on something that had really gotten under her skin, into the core of her being? This business of serving others, of being considered a responsible individual, needed. There was a peculiar satisfaction that went with all that.

Until this summer she had flitted through life concerned mostly with having fun. But this summer it had been different. Certainly there had never been a dull moment at the Center. And now, suddenly, she could no longer deny the strong pull of the hospital. She had fought it. She had almost deliberately allowed herself to "feel" for patients, and used that as an excuse for dropping the work. And yet, in spite of that she had learned to "take it." She had worked through the disaster without going to pieces. She had Miss Winters' words to prove it!

True, she had gone foolish over a boy—no, a young man, too grown-up for her. And yet, right now she found herself able to stand away and look at that situation, reasonably, dispassionately—almost with amusement. Poor David, she thought, and felt as if in that moment she had aged years. She had given him a bad time.

But now—was she really going to give up her hospital work? Involuntarily she shook her head. How could she even have thought about it seriously! There were schedule arrangements for after school work at the Center, or for Saturday or Sunday duty. She would check into those, and perhaps one day, she too, would win a cap like Nancy's and a symbolic candle. All at once her heart felt strangely light.

The newly capped girls were renewing their pledge of service, purity, integrity; their voices firm, in unison. Bonnie found her own lips moving soundlessly with theirs, but with a special meaning that was all her own.

Then the candlelit procession began to move toward the door, each girl shielding her light carefully as she sang the recessional. And when Bonnie walked out of the Meeting Room, she felt like an entirely different girl from the one who had walked in.

She went home with the Wheelers, and she was still feeling uplifted and dedicated as she walked across their lawn toward her house.

As she approached it, a figure rose from the porch steps and for a moment Bonnie's heart lurched. Could it be——

"About time you got here!" a familiar voice growled.

"Rock!" Bonnie gasped.

"Himself, in person," Rock said, pulling her toward him. "Come here, woman." He kissed her thoroughly. "I shouldn't tell you how much I've missed you," he said huskily. "What have you been up to?"

She leaned against him, suddenly spent and grateful for his strength. Dear, loyal Rock. She

could never love him like—like David. But she
would never be ungrateful for his love.

"Bonnie! Oh—gosh. I didn't know you were
busy——" Cliff Coburn had vaulted the divid-
ing hedge and now stood flatfooted and embarrassed, with Rock glaring at him. "I saw you
coming over from the Wheelers," Cliff floun-
dered and made a move back toward the hedge.

Bonnie laughed, and her laughter was young
and free. "Hello, Cliff. Don't go away. You two
fellows know each other, don't you? Come on
in the house. I think Mom baked a cake this
afternoon."

The two boys followed her, bumping shoulders in the doorway. She stifled a giggle. How
wonderful to have them here—obviously finding her special and not too young or too old,
but exactly right!

She would be nice to Rock, and kind. But
she would not go steady with him, even though
she saw insistence in his eyes as he stared at her
above his generous slab of cake. And Cliff—
well, he was sort of a special person, with many
interests. It would be fun to know him better.
And other boys; and feel heart-whole. She saw
her infatuation for David in its proper propor-
tion—proximity—the peculiar glamour of the
hospital background—her own romanticism—
his loneliness away from home.

Oh, yes, she had grown up considerably during the summer, in just the last week, as a matter of fact. She would be better poised emotionally and socially. A new year was on the way. A year of fun and school, and helping at the Medical Center—and who knew where that might lead! She might decide to be a nurse, or a technician; even a doctor, maybe! But for now, being a Candy Striper and just living would be enough!